The Little Big Book of
ROSES

The Little Big Book of
ROSES

Edited by
NATASHA TABORI FRIED & LENA TABORI

Designed by
TIMOTHY SHANER & CHRISTOPHER MEASOM

welcome
BOOKS
NEW YORK • SAN FRANCISCO

Published in 2004 by Welcome Books®
An imprint of Welcome Enterprises, Inc.
6 West 18th Street, New York, NY 10011
Tel.: (212) 989-3200; Fax: (212) 989-3205
email: info@welcomebooks.com
www.welcomebooks.com

Publisher: Lena Tabori   *Project Director:* Natasha Tabori Fried
Designers: Timothy Shaner and Christopher Measom
Production Assistant: Kathryn Shaw
Original Text: Bethany Cassin Beckerlegge and Marsha Heckman
Recipes: Sasha Perlraver
Illustrations on pages 45–46: Kathryn Shaw

Distributed to the trade in the U.S. and Canada by
Andrews McMeel Distribution Services
U.S. Orders and Customer Service Toll-free: (800) 943-9839;
Orders-only Fax: (800) 943-9831; PUBNET S&S San Number: 200-2442
Canada Toll-free: (888) 268-3216; Orders-only Fax: (888) 849-8151

Library of Congress Cataloging-in-Publication Data on file.

ISBN 1-932183-22-1

Printed in Singapore

FIRST EDITION

1 3 5 7 9 10 8 6 4 2

Contents

Songs

Facts & Histories

Recipes

Activities

My Love is Like a Red Red Rose

My love is like a red red rose
That's newly sprung in June:
My love is like the melody
That's sweetly played in tune.

So fair art thou, my bonny lass,
So deep in love am I;
And I will love thee still, my dear,
Till a' the seas gang dry.

Till a' the seas gang dry, my dear,
And the rocks melt wi' the sun:
And I will love thee still, my dear,
While the sands o' life shall run.

And fare thee weel, my only love,
And fare thee weel awhile!
And I will come again, my love,
Tho' it were ten thousand mile.

—ROBERT BURNS

Drying Roses

Drying flowers is a great way to preserve a beautiful arrangement or save a special corsage. You can use a few dried roses from a wedding bouquet to create a collage as a keepsake of the day, or combine dried roses with other types of flowers for an arrangement that will last all year long. Choose one of these three easy ways to dry your roses, and use them for decorations, crafts, or potpourri.

Microwave

1. Cover the turntable in your microwave oven with parchment or brown paper.
2. Set the microwave to its lowest setting.
3. Cut stems to fit on the turntable. Place a few roses on the paper and microwave for one minute.
4. Check roses for moisture. Microwave for 30 seconds, then check again. Repeat in 30-second intervals until the flowers are dry.
5. Allow roses to cool before carefully removing them from the microwave.

Drying Roses

Air

The best way to dry rosebuds is in warm, dry air. Hang them upside-down, with the buds not touching each other, in a dark, dry, and well-ventilated place (like an attic). Use a string, wire, or rubber band on the stem to hang the roses from a rack, a hook in the ceiling, or clothesline. Dry roses are brittle and fragile, so handle them carefully.

Desiccant

For more open roses, desiccating is the best method. The desiccant slowly absorbs all the moisture from the flower. Desiccated roses hold their color better than air-dried ones, but they are just as delicate. Silica gel from the craft store or florist supply store, a mixture of $1/2$ Borax and $1/2$ cornmeal, or clean sand that has been fully dried in the oven all work for this method. You will need an airtight container and enough desiccant to cover your rose while it is upright.

Drying Roses

1. Cut the stem to the appropriate length for your container. Fill the container to the height of the stem and put the rose in it. Sprinkle the gel crystals (or other desiccant) over the head of the rose, making sure you get the silica in between the petals, then completely cover the flower.
2. Seal the container.
3. Keep the rose in the container for 10 days at room temperature. (Note the directions on the silica package. Some gels turn pink when they have absorbed their maximum of moisture. Then the roses need to be checked for dryness, and sometimes new silica must be added.)
4. Remove the rose from the silica very carefully and gently shake off the crystals. The silica can be dried and reused.

Little Known Rose Facts

One of the oldest roses is the Gallica, or French rose.

The rose's much-adored aroma comes from the essential oil on its petals. As the flower opens, these volatile oils evaporate and perfume the air around it.

The scent of a rose is impossible to synthetically reproduce, making rose oil one of the most expensive essential oils. It can take as many as 60,000 flowers to extract just one ounce of oil.

Another name for a secret meeting is a *sub rosa*, a name derived from the ancient practice of assembling under overhanging roses.

Little Known Rose Facts

The middle name of Empress Josephine, wife of Napoleon, was Rose. She grew roses enthusiastically at her palace and sponsored the development of new hybrids.

The Romans loved roses and imported them from Egypt to use on important occasions. They gave rose wreaths to signify military success, and the winners at the Olympic games had rose petals scattered at their feet. Drawings of rose gardens were made on the walls of the catacombs to symbolize the paradise of the next world. Roses were also used at funerals, and the Romans made symbolic offerings of rosebuds to the dead during the feast of Rosalia.

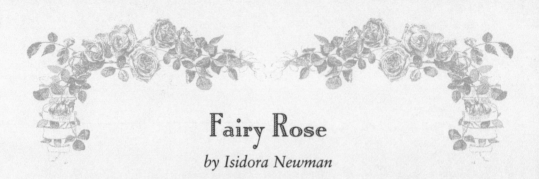

Fairy Rose

by Isidora Newman

*There are hundreds of roses in the flower world but
none lovelier in fragrance and form than the la France rose,
which is a delicate shade of pink. When the petals uncurl they
are heart-shaped and they also resemble a sea shell.*

Sunsets and sunsets ago, before the world appreciated the undawned glories of nature's mystical garden, Fairy-Rose budded and bloomed into a blossom of perfect delight. Her pink, shell-like petals opened with the perfume of dew showers.

In the early dawning hours of a beautiful spring day, a-sparkle with sunshine and a-glitter with happiness, Fairy-Rose's petal-hearts fell in love with the Sun's youthful armor-bearers, the little sprites who keep the golden armor of the Sun-god shining so brightly, and protect him from all invaders; for who can look into the face of the Sun and discover the mystery of his majesty?

These warm rays flushed with sun-bloom the tender petal-hearts of Fairy-Rose, causing them from excess of joy to droop down—down to the soft green plush of the grass carpet about her.

As Fairy-Rose lost her drooping petal-hearts, they were wafted by

Fairy Rose

sweet breezes down to the bottom of the sea, where they were soon transformed into enchanting fairy shells.

Many tides, marking the passage of days and years, had come and gone, when slowly there arose on the heaving breast of the ocean a beautiful emerald-carpeted isle, like a glittering, radiant jewel, raised by the Sea-god Neptune from his sunken marine playground.

This Magic Isle was girdled by laughing, dancing, prancing waves of blue and silver. It overflowed with joy and delight in the presence of such sparkling beauty.

The emerald island reveled in this joyous reception given her, and to add to her enchantment, she soon brought forth a lovely, shimmering pink-pearl shell for the waves and winds to caress and frolic about.

From out of the opal mist spun over this isle of fascination, the music of fairy voices chanted to the sea when lo! from the fairyshell's heart sprang Venus, the goddess of Love and Beauty.

She was indeed wondrous to gaze upon! Her alluring presence soon caused unseen spirits to fly from realms unknown to this new found isle of loveliness and light.

Silently they hovered around her throne—

The Angel of Love
And the lily-white Dove,

messengers, both eager to do the bidding of the goddess in carrying joy and gladness to all parts of this Magic Island.

Then Venus sent these spirits to gather the petal-hearts of Fairy-Rose. They flew over the jade-tinted waves and gathered these petal-hearts, one by one, stringing them magically into a rose-scepter for their wondrous Queen.

Fairy-Rose was happy to feel her petal-hearts turning into a flower scepter, and bade all the fairy friends to gather round the magic wand of Venus.

As the fair Queen of Love swayed her fragrant wand, a gorgeous golden butterfly, lost in admiration, fluttered near. He rested like a burnished diadem on the sun-beamed crown of Venus, where he remained a willing and happy captive.

Many Fairy-Roses now rejoice when they see their shell petal-hearts droop one by one, for they know they will drift to an invisible isle of love and delight. There, perhaps, they too will be gathered and clustered magically to adorn the top of the graceful rose-scepter, to be waved at the sweet will of their gracious Queen.

They seem to have whispered their pledge eternal to earthly beings, who love the music which the great composer Wagner created in "Tannhäuser," where he takes us to the Court of Venus with thousands of Fairy-Roses. We, too, love the pictures

Fairy Rose

which artists like Botticelli have painted of the Venus of that far-away Magic Island, with the golden butterfly and the shimmering, pink, fairy sea-shells and fairy rose-wand. These have been made from reflections seen in the mysterious sea, but mortal eye has never been able to discover this secret realm of Venus.

The Angel of Love
And the lily-white Dove

are always at her side, happy servitors, to protect her from earthly invasion of this Magic Isle, though if you hold her sea-shell to your ears, you too can hear the fairy music.

Thus, in the heart of every Fairy-Rose are delicate shell tracings, and in the soul of every Fairy-Rose are golden sun-spots, which are seen only after the petals have dropped away. To mortals not versed in fairy flower lore, these are but stamens; but to fairy flower friends they are golden sun-spots, nestling deep in the fragrant heart of Fairy-Rose.

Song

Weep, as if you thought of laughter!
Smile, as tears were coming after!
Marry your pleasures to your woes;
And think life's green well worth its rose!

No sorrow will your heart betide,
Without a comfort by its side;
The sun may sleep in his sea-bed,
But you have starlight overhead.

Trust not to Joy! The rose of June,
When opened wide, will wither soon;
Italian days without twilight
Will turn them suddenly to night.

Joy, most changeful of all things,
Flits away on rainbow wings;
And when they look the gayest know
It is that they are spread to go!

—ELIZABETH BARRETT BROWNING

Like the rose I, too, was careless
in the morning dews . . .

—Edith Sitwell

EVERYTHING'S COMING UP ROSES

Lyrics by Stephen Sondheim

Things look swell, Things look great,
Gonna have the whole world on a plate.
Starting here, starting now, honey,
Everything's coming up roses!
Clear the decks, clear the tracks,
We've got nothing to do but relax,
Blow a kiss, take a bow, honey,
Everything's coming up roses!

Now's our inning,
Stand the world on its ear!
Set it spinning
That'll be just the beginning!

Curtain up, light the lights,
We got nothing to hit but the heights!

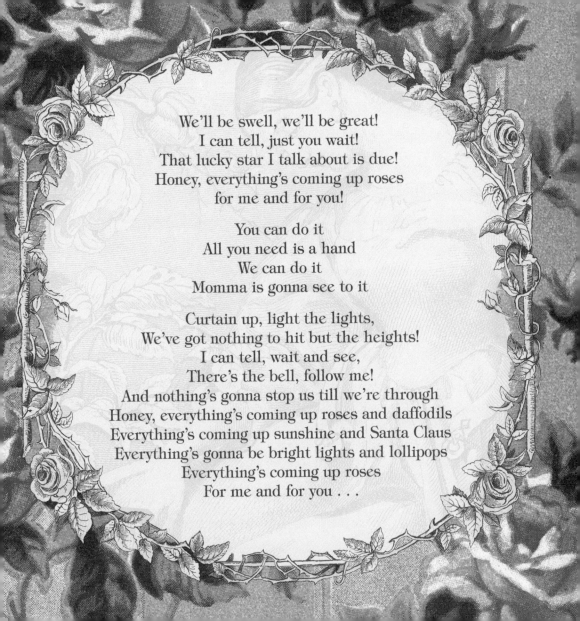

We'll be swell, we'll be great!
I can tell, just you wait!
That lucky star I talk about is due!
Honey, everything's coming up roses
for me and for you!

You can do it
All you need is a hand
We can do it
Momma is gonna see to it

Curtain up, light the lights,
We've got nothing to hit but the heights!
I can tell, wait and see,
There's the bell, follow me!
And nothing's gonna stop us till we're through
Honey, everything's coming up roses and daffodils
Everything's coming up sunshine and Santa Claus
Everything's gonna be bright lights and lollipops
Everything's coming up roses
For me and for you . . .

Rosy Outlook

by Henry Mitchell

The most overpowering time of year in my garden is when the rambler and climbing roses bloom. Not even azaleas, not even masses of tall bearded irises, produce such a sense of opulence, and this is no doubt because the masses of bloom are borne from ground level to fifteen feet in the air.

Also, unexpected combinations of color appear as you walk about the garden, thus seeing different roses as the perspective changes. The best time of day is eight or nine in the morning or after five-thirty in the afternoon. Few flowers look their best in the heat of the day, and roses are no exception.

I am quite satisfied as I walk the hundred or so feet from the kitchen to the alley. First, to the left is a bush of the rugosa rose 'Belle Poitevine,' a fragrant blowsy pink bush with a good bit of blue in the rose color. Just ahead and nearer the walk is a twelve-foot-high bush of the rugosa 'Mrs. Anthony Waterer,' bred from the highly perfumed old hybrid perpetual 'Général Jacqueminot,' as fragrant as its parent. At its full height it leans into a fragrant white rambler, 'Seagull,' which clothes an arch over the walk. A few feet beyond is the nineteenth-century creamy white, fragrant rambler 'Aglaia,' with the scentless purple rambler

Rosy Outlook

'Violette' growing into it from the other side. The white is almost finished before the purple blooms. Their flowering overlaps only a few days.

'Aglaia' has clusters of double flowers that open all together in such a mass that the leaves are hidden, as is true of most old ramblers. But 'Seagull' opens its semidouble clusters of inch-wide dead white flowers little by little, giving a starry-night effect for several days until the whole plant is solid white.

Beyond, on either side of the walk, are fat bushes about seven feet high of the white hybrid musk 'Moonlight,' which blooms off and on till frost. To the sides, thirty feet off, is the large-flowered climber 'Madame Grégoire Staechelin,' with ruffled, perfumed flowers showing a deeper rose on the reverse of the petals.

Next there is another arch with 'Blarii No. 2' on it. This is an old Bourbon rose that should not be on a small arch over a walk but should be given a stout post to grow on, with room to spread out. Its medium pink, fragrant petals are jammed into a circle, and the outer rim is almost white. The rambler

Rosy Outlook

'Violette' grows on the other side of the arch and mingles with it.

Beyond is a final arch with the single scentless bush rose 'Mutabilis' on one side and a great swag of 'Seagull' on the other, drooping over from its position in a tall yew.

The other side of the yew is support for 'Mrs. F. W. Flight,' a scented pink rambler that has large clusters of semi-double flowers. It is the pink rose grown on the tall pylons at the Roseraie de l'Haÿ outside of Paris.

After the last arch is the modern climber 'Blossomtime,' with hybrid tea-type blooms of pink, the outer petals paler. It has the good habit of casting its fragrance, and it blooms till November off and on.

On some timbers across the walk is the old noisette rose 'Jaune Desprez,' which was offered about 1830 as the first yellow climber, but in our springs it is pinkish apricot with a touch of orange. It is intensely fragrant, and beyond it is the old rambler 'The Garland,' with unbelievable masses of small white perfumed flowers in great clusters.

To one side, tangling with it, is the Bourbon 'Variegata di Bologna,' extremely double and intensely scented light pink blooms striped with crimson-purple. It grows into the white rambler and on into a red cedar.

Some of these roses are popular, at least in famous gardens, and others not. To the extreme left of these is a white multiflora rambler that you might think is the wild *Rosa multiflora*, but my friend Nicholas Weber points out various differences. It has the overwhelming fragrance of the multiflora and came from the garden of the late Mrs. Frederick Keays in Maryland, the woman who did much to start the interest in old roses decades ago.

Far to the right against a fence is 'Polyantha Grandiflora,' a larger, glossier variant on the multiflora, and running in back of it are the white 'Madame Plantier' and some albas.

Most of these roses bloom only in spring and only for a couple of weeks. When they bloom I feel I have all the roses I want, so massive is their flowering. I may have missed a few along the way: the yellow, strangely scented 'Agnes,' deep red 'Dr. Huey,' the perfumed pink rambler 'Ginny,' the barely scented scarlet 'Will Scarlet.' It might be more tasteful to have less of this mass flowering, but if you want to feel drowned in roses, these are the kinds that will do it. 🍃

Roses

Nature responds so beautifully.
Roses are only once-wild roses, that
were given an extra chance,
So they bloomed out and filled
themselves with colored fullness

Out of sheer desire to be splendid,
and more splendid.

—D. H. LAWRENCE

Candied Rose Petals

Candied rose petals should be stored in an airtight container in a cool, dry place with each layer separated by both wax paper and a paper towel. Moisture is your enemy! These would be lovely as decoration on the Rose Cake (see page 154).

2 EGG WHITES, BEATEN
1 CUP GRANULATED SUGAR
24 ORGANIC ROSE PETALS

1. Begin by inspecting your rose petals carefully. They should be clean and unblemished.
2. Beat egg whites in a shallow bowl until they are frothy.
3. Place sugar in a separate shallow bowl.
4. Using a clean pastry brush or soft tweezers, gently coat a single rose petal, first in egg white, then in sugar, on both sides.
5. Lay each finished rose petal on wax paper and allow to dry.

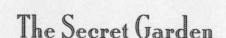

The Secret Garden

by Frances Hodgson Burnett

She was standing *inside* the secret garden.

It was the sweetest, most mysterious-looking place anyone could imagine. The high walls which shut it in were covered with the leafless stems of climbing roses, which were so thick that they were matted together. Mary Lennox knew they were roses because she had seen a great many roses in India. All the ground was covered with grass of wintry brown, and out of it grew clumps of bushes which were surely rose-bushes if they were alive. There were numbers of standard roses which had so spread their branches that they were like little trees. There were other trees in the garden, and one of the things that made the place look strangest and loveliest was that climbing roses had run all over them and swung down long tendrils which made light swaying curtains, and here and there they had caught at each other or at a far-reaching branch and had crept from one tree to another and made lovely bridges of themselves. There were neither leaves nor roses on them now, and Mary did not know whether they were dead or alive, but their thin grey or brown branches and sprays looked like a sort of hazy mantle spreading over everything, walls, and trees, and even brown grass, where they had felled from their fastenings, and run along the ground. It was this hazy tangle from tree to tree which made it look so mysterious. Mary had thought it must be different from other gardens which had not been left all by themselves so long; and, indeed, it was different from any other place she had ever seen in her life . . . and she felt she had found a world all her own.

I saw a rosebud ope
this morn; I'll swear
The blushing morning
opened not more fair.

—Abraham Cowley

Choosing Healthy Roses

Nothing is more frustrating than faithfully tending your roses, only to be rewarded by poor growth and flower production. Choosing robust plants from the start can make all the difference in the vitality of your roses. Use these tips to pick the best roses for you, and grow vigorous, healthy blooms all summer long.

1 Research which roses are vigorous growers in your zone and which ones are most disease resistant. By choosing plants known for their ability to fend off fungus and pests, you increase your chances of growing a healthy, beautiful plant. See "Carefree Roses" on page 229 for a list of hardy breeds.

2 Choose plants that match the kind of garden-er you are. If you are willing to devote a lot of time to your roses, you can choose more exotic and delicate varieties that require constant attention. On the other hand, if you have a thumb that's not entirely green, pick roses that need little more than a sunny spot, good soil, gentle water-ing, and occasional feeding and pruning.

Choosing Healthy Roses

3 Consider once-blooming roses over repeat-bloomers. Species roses and old garden roses like Albas and rugosas that bloom once a season are generally more disease resistant than their repeat-blooming counterparts. After blooming, the foliage on once-blooming roses goes through a period of hardening to prepare for winter. The waxy foliage and tougher stems protect the rose from fungus and disease. Repeat-blooming roses produce tender new shoots all the time, making them more susceptible to pests.

4 Buy No.-1-grade plants. When purchasing bareroot roses from a mail-order nursery, spend the extra money to get No. 1 grade. A No.-1-grade plant will have at least three large branches and intact roots that are healthy and strong. The increased vigor of these plants is well worth the extra cost. Spending less on a 1 1/2- or 2-grade plant could lead to more work on your part and perhaps a disappointing rose.

5 Consider buying own-root roses. Nurseries that offer roses grown on their own root stock as opposed to just the grafted variety most likely have a great interest in the health and heartiness

Choosing Healthy Roses

of their plants. Roses grown on their own roots tend to be vigorous and disease-free. While there are many healthy varieties of grafted roses, viral diseases can be transmitted through the grafting process, so be sure to ask if the rootstock of a grafted plant is certified virus-free.

6 If you are purchasing container-grown roses for your garden, chose plants with glossy, dark green, and disease-free foliage. The roses should have a well-balanced structure of healthy canes and a firm, well-watered root-ball. Choose plants that already show a number of flower buds. Avoid roses that are dropping leaves— this could be a sign of drought, vitamin and mineral deficiencies, or disease.

Shapes of the Rose

When you picture a rose in your mind, no doubt the vision is of a perfect hybrid tea in your favorite color (red, perhaps?) But roses come in many shapes and sizes; some blooms burst with petals, while others delicately unfold only five. These illustrations show the beautiful range of the rose in

FLAT: This type of flower is usually found on species roses and contains five petals opening to a round gathering of stamens in the middle.

HIGH CENTERED: A shape most often associated with hybrid tea roses, the petals in this flower rise to a high center and make a point.

Shapes of the Rose

LOOSELY DOUBLED: With anywhere from six to twenty-five petals, this flower shape appears most often in floribundas or hybrid teas.

QUARTERED: Almost flat, this rose is packed with petals divided into four distinct sections.

ROSETTE: This nearly flat shape is bursting with overlapping and unevenly spaced petals.

URN SHAPED: The petals on this rose are flat on the outside, but curve up to an urn shape in the middle.

Time of Roses

It was not in the winter
Our loving lot was cast!
It was the time of roses,
We plucked them as we passed.

That churlish season never frowned
On early lovers yet!
Oh no—the world was newly crowned
With flowers, when first we met.

'Twas twilight, and I bade you go,
But still you held me fast;
It was the time of roses,
We plucked them as we passed!

What else could peer my glowing cheek
That tears began to stud?
And when I asked the like of Love
You snatched a damask bud,

And oped it to the dainty core
Still glowing to the last:
It was the time of roses,
We plucked them as we passed.

—THOMAS HOOD

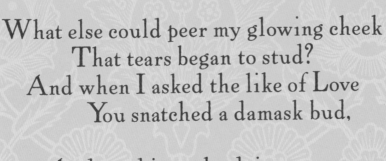

'Alchymist'

by Jamaica Kincaid

Is this a good thing for me to be doing, actually putting into writing the idea that I have a favorite rose? Do I have a favorite rose? Does anybody? How can anybody like one rose above all others? There are so many roses to begin with, and then there are even more. When people meet roses, they fall in love with them so much that a whole process of tampering is set in motion. And yet there is one rose I love and would be very sorry not to have growing in my garden.

My favorite rose, then, is 'Alchymist.' Its provenance is 'Golden Glow' and an unspecified *R. egalnteria* hybrid. It came into my life in this way: I was at the most feeble and ignorant stage of my gardening life—I was at the beginning. The house I live in now was new to me. It had some old flower beds, planted with peonies (big red-maroon things), roses (small pink fragrant blossoms that came at once in early June and that was that), and some daylilies (*Hemerocallis fulva*). Without hesitating, I began to move some things here, other things there, and when I grew tired of that, I dug up and threw away the rest. How I regret that now, the throwing-away part. Especially I regret throwing away all those roses. But in those days, I approached the garden with great certainty—not confidence, just certainty—that everything I did and thought was so clearly the right thing to do. I certainly did not like flowers that bloomed fleetingly, and I would not grow them.

In those days, I made many trips each day to places where garden things could be purchased. I would find that I needed things to make the soil more sweet and things to make the soil more sour; something that would make a plant produce more leaves and something that would make it bear more fruit. I was so much at the store getting things to make a plant do what a plant will do, I often forgot that a plant knew how to do anything at all by itself. I never went to the garden store to buy plants; I bought most of my plants through the mail. I went to the garden store to buy things that are meant to support plants.

But, of course, one of the unfortunate things about gardening is how it puts you in an acquisitive mood. So it was that on one of those many trips to the garden store I bought something that I had not gone to the garden store to buy in the first place. I saw two rosebushes in five-gallon pots, and, without knowing what kind of rosebushes they were, I bought them. They cost me almost ten dollars each.

One of the roses turned out to be a 'Henry Kelsey' (a nice red rose that seems to enjoy a fair amount of mistreatment, which it gets from me both on purpose and accidentally), and the other was the now much-

'Alchymist'

loved and treasured 'Alchymist.' I planted them and replanted them a few times before I was satisfied that I had gotten rose planting right. The year after, 'Henry Kelsey' bloomed but 'Alchymist' did not.

That first year, when 'Alchymist' did not bloom, I was on the verge of uprooting it and placing it in that netherworld of plants tossed out. But I saved the rose and the tag that came with it, a little piece of stiff paper on which appeared the words "R. Alchymist," and next to that a picture of a peach-colored, open-faced flower, my rose. Over the next couple of years, many things happened. I found that I had started to make a garden without meaning to do so, for one thing. I thought I was just putting plants in the ground in a way that pleased me, but almost behind my own back, certainly without any true purpose, I was making a garden. All that time, while the 'Alchymist' just sat there, throwing out ten-foot-long cane after ten-foot-long cane, making the act of growing seem a form of languishing, I got all sorts of ideas about the garden, and they were not limited to shady and sunny, hardy and tender. I came to know the garden as the place where conquest becomes a beautiful distraction. The rose all by itself is a splendid example: some of them come to us from someplace Alexander the Great passed through, some of them come to us through the travels of a priest, and so forth.

I had just begun to make my way in the garden, but was quite full of myself and my little observations, and not at all afraid to declare them. This made many gardeners I knew who had been laboring for many years

'Alchymist'

resentful. One day I was having a conversation with a gardener I knew and admired for her delphiniums. When I told her of the ease I had growing them, she told me the error I had been making that led to this ease. I was properly chastened, but at parting, perhaps feeling I needed a little more chastisement, I told her that I had planted the rose 'Alchymist' and how worried I was about it, for it had never bloomed. My friend told me that of course this rose would never bloom for me, it was not meant for my climate, too tender, my cold winters would kill the old canes. Didn't I know that 'Alchymist' blooms on old canes? How sad it was that I did not know more about the things I had planted in my garden, how sad it was that I did not know more about the garden in general, how lucky I was to know someone who knew more about the garden than I did.

Feeling properly humbled, I went home and looked at my rose. I was sad. Implied in my friend's sturdy and authoritative advice was the notion that I should give up the idea of cultivating this particular rose altogether; that I should find another rose (the suggestion was 'Roseraie de l'Haÿ') that would suit the cold southern-Vermont climate in which I live. But I have never liked people telling me what to do. When I am told what to do, I do its opposite, even when what I am told to do is the right thing to do.

Three years after I planted the 'Alchymist,' it bloomed. When I first detected its buds, I thought it was coming down with an illness I had not yet read about, so accustomed had I become to seeing canes of leaves and thorns. As the buds grew bigger, I was sure my plant was dying. In

'Alchymist'

hours (twenty-four to thirty-six) they went from bud to flower—
yellow, peach, or pink, depending on how my eye perceived those colors or what light they were seen in.

This difficult distinction, between pure perception and what influences
my perception, captures the distinct nature of this rose, for 'Alchymist' is
never a model of stability. It will sometimes seem to go from yellow to
peach to pink, or start out pink and go to yellow and then peach. It
starts out as if it will be the usual tea rose, and then it develops into the
fullest quartered rose I have ever seen. Every description of it I have read
says it is scented, even highly scented. Mine have no scent at all. I have
five plants growing in different parts of the garden, each of them bought
from a different place, and they all have the same
characteristic unpredictability and no fragrance at
all. The absence of fragrance is strong.

That my favorite rose is one that I am not
supposed to be able to grow and that by its
nature is not predictable does not surprise
me. I take it as a given that all things worth
loving are difficult, hard to pin down, and
changeable, all the while being true to
themselves. The 'Alchymist' can do whatever it wants, but it remains a rose, the
rose that I love. 🍃

Then I will raise aloft
the milk-white rose,
For whose sweet
smell the air shall
be perfumed.

—William Shakespeare

A White Rose

The red rose whispers of passion,
And the white rose breathes of love;
O, the red rose is a falcon,
And the white rose is a dove.

But I send you a cream-white rosebud
With a flush on its petal tips;
For the love that is purest and sweetest
Has a kiss of desire on the lips.

—JOHN BOYLE O'REILLY

ROSE SYRUP

Delicately flavored Rose Syrup, called "dew of Paradise" in the Middle East, can be bought in specialty groceries that carry Middle Eastern, Greek, Turkish, and Indian foods. It is mainly used in dessert recipes and to sweeten drinks. Add a spoonful to hot or iced tea, lemonade, or whipped cream. Drizzle some on grapefruit. Rose syrup also blends well with chocolate, coffee, fruit, and nuts.

1 QUART ORGANIC ROSE PETALS
3 CUPS SUGAR
3/4 CUP COLD WATER

1. Wash the rose petals and dry them with a paper towel. Tear or cut off the white tip at the base of the petals, called the heel, which tastes bitter.

2. Spread the petals on a dry, clean cloth and allow them to dry for 1 or 2 days.
3. Place the rose petals in a saucepan and cover with 1 cup of sugar.
4. Crush the petals into the sugar using a wide, wooden spoon. Bruise the petals thoroughly.
5. Add the water and bring the mixture to a boil. Gradually add the rest of the sugar, dissolving it completely.
6. Boil slowly while stirring constantly until syrup is formed.
7. Strain into a sterile jar or bottle. Cover tightly and store for 2 weeks before using.

FOR A DELICIOUS DESSERT: Pour rose syrup over slices of oranges, pears, nectarines, and strawberries. Marinate for 2 hours. Garnish with mint and serve with almond cookies and fruit sorbet or almond ice cream. Store the syrup in a tightly sealed container in the refrigerator and it will keep for a few months.

Snow White and Rose Red

by The Brothers Grimm

Once upon a time there was a poor widow who had two lovely daughters. They were named Snow White and Rose Red, after the blooms on the two rose trees in front of their cottage. The girls were best friends, and did everything together. They would run through the meadow, finding flowers for their mother, or they would frolic in the forest, gathering berries and making friends with all the woodland creatures. When it was time for their chores, they worked to keep their mother's cottage neat and tidy. On summer mornings, Rose Red made a wreath of flowers to lay by her mother's bed. On winter evenings, Snow White lit the fire and hung the brightly polished kettle to warm. The sisters would sit by the fire, while their mother read to them.

Every night before going to bed, Snow White said, "We must always be together."

Her sister replied, "As long as we live."

Their mother would add, "What one has, she must share with the other."

One evening someone knocked at the door. Rose Red eagerly jumped up to answer it. But when she unbolted the door, a big, black bear

Snow White and Rose Red

nosed his way into their cottage. Rose Red was startled, and ran. Snow White took cover under her mother's bed. But this was no ordinary bear. He began to speak. "Please don't be afraid," he said. "I mean you no harm. I am half-frozen, and only wish to get warm."

"Poor bear," said the mother, "lie down by the fire, but be careful not to burn your coat." Then she called, "Snow White, Rose Red, come out. The bear is our guest and our friend."

So the sisters came out, and soon grew comfortable with their new furry friend. They even made a fun routine of his nightly visits: He would come at the same time each night, and they would bring out the broom and sweep the snow from his coat. Then he would stretch out by the fire and let out a great yawn. But the sisters wouldn't let him sleep right away. They tugged his fur, rolled him about, and took turns riding on his back. He would pretend to growl and they would laugh. Sometimes, when they were too rough with the bear, he said, "Please let me live! Are you trying to beat your suitor to death?"

When the snow began to melt away, and the earliest spring flowers were popping through the soil, the bear announced to Snow White that it was time for him to go away for a while. This made her very sad, because she had grown rather fond of the bear. "I must leave you until the leaves fall from the trees," he said. "Then I will return to continue our courtship." Snow White laughed and blushed.

"But where are you going?" she asked.

Snow White and Rose Red

"I must return to the forest to protect my treasure from the wicked dwarfs," he explained. "When the earth is frozen, they must stay underground in their caves. But in the spring, they break through to the surface and search for treasure."

They said their good-byes, and the bear trotted across the yard and was soon out of sight.

A few days later, their mother sent Snow White and Rose Red to the forest to collect firewood. They walked until they found a great tree that had fallen across a stream. Near the base of the tree something was moving. As they got closer, they saw that it was an old dwarf with a long, white beard. The end of his beard was caught in the tree. "Well don't just stand there, you silly girls!" shouted the dwarf. "Help me!"

The girls were shocked, but they tried in vain to pull him free.

"How did you ever get yourself caught in a tree?" asked Rose Red.

"What's it to you, anyway?" snarled the dwarf.

"Well, I should go find someone to help," she said.

"Why?" asked the dwarf. "You two are already two too many for me! Can't you senseless geese think of something?"

"Don't be so impatient," said Snow White. "I have an idea." She pulled her scissors from her pocket and cut off the end of the dwarf's beard.

"You're more stupid than I thought," said the dwarf. "Cutting a piece from my fine beard will give you bad luck for a year!"

Then the dwarf grabbed a small sack filled with gold, which had been

Snow White and Rose Red

lying in the roots of the tree, and ran off with it.

So Snow White and Rose Red gathered some firewood and headed home. They followed the stream until again they found the dwarf jumping about like a grass-hopper. "Well don't just stand there, you foolish girls!" shouted the dwarf. "Help me! This pesky fish at the end of my line wants to pull me in. I would let him go, but the wind has gotten my beard tangled in my line."

The sisters grabbed hold of the little man and tried again in vain to free his beard. Snow White brought out her scissors and cut the beard loose. The dwarf screamed out, "Are you crazy? It wasn't enough that you snipped off the end of my beard. Now you had to cut the best part of it. Your bad luck will never end." Then he picked up a sack of pearls from the tall grass, and without another word, he dragged it away.

The next day, the sisters went to the town on errands. They noticed a large bird circling high above their heads. The bird swooped down, and they heard a loud cry. The girls ran over and saw the eagle held their old acquaintance the dwarf in its talons, and was trying to carry him off. They took hold of him and pulled until the eagle finally let go. "Couldn't you have been more careful?" cried the dwarf. "You practically pulled my coat apart, you clumsy creatures!" Then he grabbed a sack full of precious stones and crept into his cave. The sisters, who were used to his thanklessness, continued on to town.

On their way home they surprised the dwarf, who had emptied his bag

Snow White and Rose Red

onto the road. The sun lit up the brilliant stones, and they glittered and sparkled so beautifully that the girls stood and stared at them. "Get away from here, you dreadful beings!" the dwarf said in a rage.

Suddenly, a loud growling came from the forest, and a black bear came trotting toward them. The terrified dwarf ran, but he could not reach his cave in time. He cried out, "Dear Mister Bear, please spare my life. I will give you all these beautiful jewels. You don't want to eat me, anyway. Take these two tasty girls instead." The bear killed the wicked creature with a single strike of his paw.

The sisters started to run, but the bear called to them, "Snow White and Rose Red, don't be afraid." They recognized their friend's voice and turned to see the bear had disappeared. Standing in his place was a handsome man, clothed in gold. "I am a king's son," he said, "and that wicked dwarf stole my treasures and put a curse on me. I have had to live in the forest as a bear until I was freed by his death. Now he has received his fair reward."

The prince took Snow White to his kingdom, where he married her, and Rose Red married his brother. They shared the great treasure the dwarf had collected. Their mother lived happily with her children for many years. She brought the two rose trees with her, and they grew before her window. Every year, they produced the most beautiful roses—white and red.

Rose Water

The wife of an Indian Raj, Empress Nur Mahal, is given credit for inventing rose water in the seventeenth century. She discovered that rose petals would release their heavenly fragrance when soaked in water. Rose water, called atterdane, became an important part of Indian rituals. To this day, Indian brides enjoy a ritual bath in rose water before the marriage ceremony and rose water is poured from a brass pitcher called aftaba to cleanse one's hands before and after a special meal.

In Persia, rose petals are simply placed in a vessel with rainwater and left in the sun for several days.

Commercial roses are not suitable for making rose water. Use only garden roses that have not been sprayed with any chemicals. The best time to cut roses is in the morning after the dew has dried. Pick fragrant roses that are open but not yet faded. Remove the petals, and rinse them clean of any dirt and insects.

To make about a quart of distilled rose water you will need two to three quarts of fragrant rose petals (petals from 4 to 6 dozen roses), water, ice, a clean brick, a 1-quart heatproof bowl, a large pot, and a stainless steel bowl big enough to cover the pot. (If you use a canning pot with a domed lid, you can invert the lid and use it to hold the ice.)

1. Place the brick in the pot and surround it with the rose petals. Cover the petals with bottled or purified water to just above the top of the brick. Put the 1-quart bowl on top of the brick.
2. Bring the water to a boil, then turn heat down to a low simmer.
3. Place the large bowl on top of the pot and fill it with ice. Keep adding ice the whole time you are distilling the mixture.
4. The rose-infused steam will collect on the bottom of the steel bowl, and drip into the small bowl as it is cooled by the ice.
5. Simmer the rose petal and water mixture over very low heat for 1 to 2 hours. Check constantly to make sure the water does not cook away.
6. Empty the small bowl of rose water every 30 minutes into a clean covered container. Store the rose water in the refrigerator.

RED IS THE ROSE

Come over the hills, my bonnie Irish lass
Come over the hills to your darling
You choose the rose, love, and I'll make the vow
And I'll be your true love forever.

Chorus
Red is the rose that in yonder garden grows
Fair is the lily of the valley
Clear is the water that flows from the Boyne
But my love is fairer than any.

'Twas down by Killarney's green woods that we strayed
When the moon and the stars they were shining
The moon shone its rays on her locks of golden hair
And she swore she'd be my love forever.

Chorus
It's not for the parting that my sister pains
It's not for the grief of my mother
'Tis all for the loss of my bonny Irish lass
That my heart is breaking forever.

Gather Ye Rosebuds

Gather ye rosebuds while ye may,
Old Time is still a-flying:
And this same flower that smiles today
Tomorrow will be dying.

The glorious lamp of heaven, the sun,
The higher he's a-getting,
The sooner will his race be run,
And nearer he's to setting.

That age is best which is the first,
When youth and blood are warmer;
But being spent, the worse, and worst
Times still succeed the former.

Then be not coy, but use your time,
And while ye may, go marry:
For having lost but once your prime,
You may for ever tarry.

—ROBERT HERRICK

The Language of Roses

As one of the most revered and cultivated flowers in the world, roses have held deep meaning since antiquity. Each color connotes emotions or signifies special feelings when presented to another. Peruse this list and add a little extra meaning to the next arrangement you send, or use it to decode a secret message sent to you in roses.

ROSEBUDS denote youth and beauty; red rosebuds mean "pure and lovely," while white rosebuds symbolize girlhood. The moss rosebud stands for confessions of love.

DEEP BURGUNDY roses denote inner beauty.

THE RED ROSE symbolizes love, respect, courage, and desire.

DARK CRIMSON ROSES are given as a symbol of mourning.

ROSE LEAVES symbolize hope.

The Language of Roses

PINK represents grace, elegance, and gentleness.

DARK PINK ROSES stand for gratitude and appreciation.

LIGHT PINK ones convey admiration and sympathy.

WHITE ROSES stand for innocence, purity, reverence, and humility, but can also mean secrecy and silence.

RED AND WHITE together, or WHITE ROSES TIPPED IN RED, symbolize unity.

YELLOW ROSES denoted jealousy in Victorian times, but are now given to express friendship, joy, gladness, and freedom.

RED and YELLOW ROSES together signify happiness and joviality.

CORAL and ORANGE ROSES convey enthusiasm and desire, and say, "I am proud of you."

"BLUE" ROSES are associated with fantasy, the impossible, miracles, and new possibilities, as no blue roses truly exist in nature.

PALE PEACH ROSES are a symbol of modesty.

The Language of Roses

TWO ROSES TOGETHER on a single stem indicate engagement and upcoming marriage.

SINGLE ROSES stand for simplicity, and in full bloom mean, "I love you" or "I love you still." A bouquet of roses in full bloom is an expression of gratitude.

A CROWN MADE OF ROSES signifies virtue and reward.

A ROSE IN FULL BLOOM placed over two buds creates a combination signifying secrecy.

TEA ROSES mean that you will be remembered always.

A ROSE WITHOUT THORNS conveys love at first sight.

Raspberry Rose Water Sorbet

$1/2$ POUND FRESH RASPBERRIES
$1^{1}/_{2}$ CUPS SUGAR
1 TABLESPOON FRESH LEMON JUICE
$1/4$ CUP RED WINE
$1/4$ CUP LIGHT CORN SYRUP
$1/3$ CUP ROSE WATER (SEE PAGE 68)

1. Combine raspberries, sugar, and lemon juice.
2. Marinate for 30 minutes to 1 hour.
3. Add wine, corn syrup, and rose water, stirring to combine well.
4. Freeze in an ice cream maker according to manufacturer's instructions. Serve cold.

Yields: 1 quart

The Wild Rose-Briar

Love is like the wild rose-briar;
Friendship like the holly-tree.
The holly is dark when the rose-briar blooms,
But which will bloom most constantly?

The wild rose-briar is sweet in spring,
Its summer blossoms scent the air;
Yet wait till winter comes again,
And who will call the wild-briar fair?

Then, scorn the silly rose-wreath now,
And deck thee with the holly's sheen,
That, when December blights thy brow,
He may still leave thy garland green.

—EMILY BRONTË

Would Jove appoint some flower to reign
In matchless beauty on the plain
The Rose (Mankind will all agree)
The Rose the Queen of Flowers should b
—Sappho

Cultivating Delight

by Diane Ackerman

Beware of Shakespeare!" a man said to me recently. "You can't trust any of the characters. Othello is charming, but too fruity. Pretty Jessica is dependable, but downright common. Jacquenetta is appealing, all right, a real buxom country wench, but completely unstable. Prospero can be subtle, with an interesting spectrum of moods, but just doesn't appear for long enough. Proud Titania, when you come down to it, has too many problems to keep track of. For my money, William Shakespeare is a gaudy giant, but requires altogether too much work."

That did it. "Listen," I said, "I think they're all brilliant creation. Okay, you don't get much of Prospero, but what you do get is rich and unforgettable. Sweet Juliet has the sort of blushing extravagance I would defend to the grave!"

We were two gardeners talking about roses. Wouldn't Shakespeare be surprised to find many of his characters transmogrified in gardens all over the world? He'd probably hate the bad press the David Austin English roses with Shakespearean names are getting at the moment. And how confusing to have both a rose and a ligularia called Othello.

~

Cultivating Delight

Paradise has returned. Not minimal paradise, mind you, not the bare bones of a paradise too weak to count on, but a tough resilient paradise with thick strong limbs, erect posture, and vigorous ways. A thorny paradise. There's nothing delicate or fey about its blooming fists of lavender. "Yikes!" I say out loud, in a mixture of delight and confusion. It's like waking up to find your dead uncle returned as a heavyweight boxer standing in your garden.

A matte lavender rose sometimes edged in dark purple, Paradise is not a keeper in my locale. All of the purple and lavender roses fare poorly here, where something in their lineage makes them vulnerable to our winters. But with the weather topsy-turvy now, you never know what curio might appear to defy custom and turn local wisdom on its ear. I have scant success with the lavender Angel Face, but perhaps I'll give it another try. Unlike Paradise, Angel Face has golden majorette fringes inside when it opens, and petals delicate as veils of rain.

If I were a little girl, I suppose, I might arrange roses in a semicircle of bud vases and pretend they were dolls, because they do have faces, just as books have faces. One concern I have about the current generation of electronic books is their facelessness. Books look different, and that adds to the pleasurable illusion of carrying with you a distinctive mind. That may be remedied one day in e-books, but for the time being I respond to the personality of bindings and dust jackets. I've written at length elsewhere about the natural history of the face, and why we're driven to see faces everywhere, even on rock formations on Mars! Suffice it to say that we like to inhabit the nonhuman world with recognizable friends and fiends. I brings this up because people are sometimes chided for what's called "anthropomorphism," attributing human characteristics to nonhuman plants and animals. We've inherited that prohibition from the outdated belief that we are not animals and therefore share nothing with other animals. That leads to the assumption that we can learn nothing about human behavior by observing plants and animals. How arrogant and how foolish. Evolution has used many of the same tricks for plants, animals, and humans alike.

I love sitting at the crossroads where nature and human nature meet and earth throws light upon the other. So although I don't imagine my plants share human concerns and emotions, I do respond to their unique faces, as well as to their motives, strategies, culture, and health. Do plants have motives and instincts? Absolutely. To the best of my knowledge, they don't have consciousness. But they are self-aware. They know when they've been hurt, and they can take stock of their circumstances and adjust their behavior. For example, on frosty spring mornings, I often find tulips bent over, as if dead; but they're up again by noon. Freezing water would explode the cell walls, so to protect themselves, they

Cultivating Delight

go limp when the temperature plunges and send water down to their feet. Then they shoot water back up to the flowers when it's safe.

In times of drought some animals become nocturnal to reduce their need for water, while others—say, fish in a dried-up pond—go into a sort of hibernation until the rains come. Most plants go limp. Flowers tell you when they are thirsty. Few things are as pathetic as an impatiens shriveled up and drooping like a spaniel with its muzzle on its paws. Dry soil can leach the water out of plants, which then roll up their leaves to conserve moisture. They have a better chance of survival if they sacrifice leaves and flowers and pull all the sustenance down into the bulb or roots. They can grow new flowers and leaves, but they can't afford to lose their core. Odd though this might sound, evolution equipped women with a similar response, which I learned about in the Antarctic, whose waters are so frigid that you will die almost instantly if you fall into them. Women are in more danger than men from hypothermia because women's bodies preferentially protect the reproductive organs, and will pull blood from the brain, heart, and everywhere else to warm the reproductive core.

Plants grow feverish when they catch a virus, and they even get the equivalent of flushed cheeks. Researchers from the University of Ghent infected tobacco plants with tobacco mosaic virus, and using a high-resolution infrared cameras, discovered that leaf temperatures were higher at the sites of infection, and that the fever appeared before any visible signs of illness. The discovery will help in the early diagnosis of crop disease, but it also adds to our understanding of what we have in common with plants. They get feverish when sick, droopy when under stress.

An exuberance of roses this year. So many are blooming that I gather three dozen to bring indoors, and only stop because I've no more room in my pail. I don't remember a year when roses bloomed this lavishly. The Colette rose (firm buds like young bosoms, opening to light pink blooms with a wash of apricot) is towering up the fence, creating a flower trail as it goes. The real Colette, who wrote books in which she treats flowers and people with equal respect, would adore the fountain of pink flowers—and the unusually large thorns, too. Along one fence, four climbing rosebushes rearrange their blankets of color each day, as some blooms wither and others open. Reine de Violette, an old-fashioned bushy purple rose that unfolds into a shallow ruffle the color of grape juice, has become an avid climber for some reason, and begun streaming over the fence. Next to it a pool of deep pink roses, then a spread of orange-red roses, then an explosion of small, pale pink roses, and finally a huge flight of blue-red roses growing in bunches of five to ten buds. Behind them, a rose the darkest red I've ever seen climbs a tall black obelisk. What a display. Noses (the people who invent perfumes) refer to floral scents as notes, their combinations as chords, and in their workrooms they tend to arrange scents like the keys of a pedal organ. In the scent-music of my rose garden, there are major and minor chords, simple

Cultivating Delight

notes one can smell for a long while, and others the nose smells fleetingly, which seem to evaporate like sixteenth notes. Every rose has unique qualities, opens at its own pace, and grows into its color and scent in predictable ways. Weather is a wild card, as are flukes of breeding, so just when you start to take a rose for granted—ho-hum, another rose equivalent of a trapeze artist—nature grabs you by the lapels and wakes up your dozy senses.

Roses on the Terrace

Rose, on this terrace fifty years ago,
When I was in my June, you in your May,
Two words, 'My Rose,' set all your face aglow,
And now that I am white, and you are gray,
That blush of fifty years ago, my dear,
Blooms in the Past, but close to me today
As this red rose, which on our terrace here
Glows in the blue of fifty miles away.

—ALFRED, LORD TENNYSON

Planting Your Roses

By doing some simple preparation, you can boost your chances of growing beautiful, healthy roses right from the start. These tips will help you plant your roses correctly, and set them up for a summer of blooms!

❧

UNDERSTAND YOUR PLANT: Bareroot roses need to be planted in early spring, once the danger of frost has passed. Container roses can be planted anytime, from early spring until the end of the summer. Look at a bareroot rose to see whether the plant is an own-root rose or a grafted rose. The trunk of a rose grown on its own rootstock will be from one to four inches long, and straight with canes branching from it. Grafted roses have a bump on the trunk called the graft union, the place where the graft was made on the original rootstock. The graft union is the most sensitive part of your rose, so you will have to take care of it accordingly.

❧

INSPECT THE MERCHANDISE: When your bareroot roses arrive, examine them carefully. Use pruning shears to trim off broken roots and wipe off any white mold. Cut back all of the

Planting Your Roses

roots about a half inch to promote new growth. Now look at the canes, or top growth. Trim off damaged or deadwood, and then cut them back so that they are about eight to twelve inches tall. By cutting the canes short, you give your rose a chance to develop a healthy root system before it uses energy supporting the top growth.

❧

HYDRATE! Your bareroot roses will be very thirsty after their journey. Fill a bucket with water, add some vitamin B1 (you can find this at your local nursery) and submerge your plants, canes and all, for up to 24 hours. Another method to keep them fortified and hydrated is to soak them in a mixture of equal parts soil and manure, with enough water added to make it pourable. Keep them in the mixture for an hour, then remove them. The mud will dry caked on the roots to form a protective coating that will nourish them and encourage growth.

❧

CHOOSE THE RIGHT SPOT, AND DIG: Most experts recommend digging a hole about two feet deep by two feet in diameter in well-drained soil. Place the top 12 inches of soil (topsoil) off to the side and finish digging the hole. Mix soil taken from the lower part of the hole with an equal-size helping of compost and set aside.

❧

Planting Your Roses

PLANTING BAREROOT ROSES: Make a mound at the bottom of the hole with topsoil and rest the bareroot rose at the top, spreading the roots out over the mound. Be sure that the graft union will be three to five inches below ground. Fill the rest of the hole with the soil and compost mixture about three inches from the surface and water thoroughly. Fill the hole completely and top off with mulch to protect the canes.

PLANTING CONTAINER ROSES: The process is similar. First, set your potted rose in water to hydrate the root-ball while you dig the hole. Carefully remove the plant from the container, making sure to keep the root-ball intact. Place the rose on a mound of topsoil in the hole (as with bareroot roses) and adjust so that the graft union will be below ground when planted. Fill in the hole with the compost and soil mixture to about three inches from the surface, water well, and mulch.

KEEP AN EYE ON YOUR NEW ROSES: Check them often to see if they need water. If you stick your finger an inch into the soil and it feels dry, it's time to water. Be sure to water deeply and hold off from fertilizing for at least a month to give your roots time to grow.

What is fairer than a rose?
What is sweeter?

—George Herbert

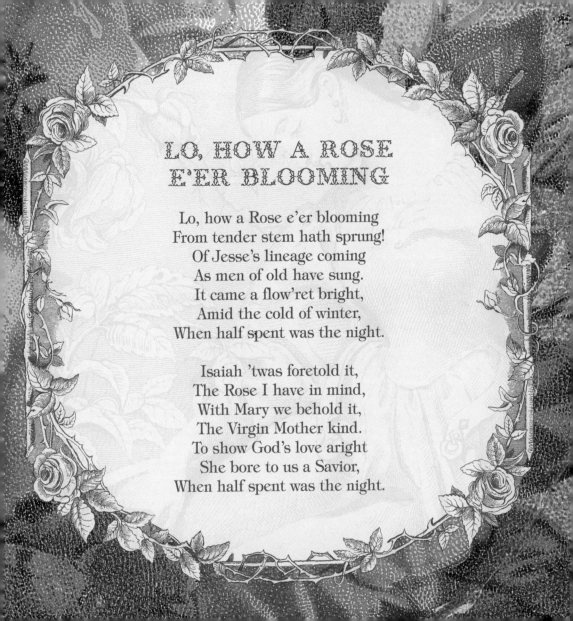

LO, HOW A ROSE
E'ER BLOOMING

Lo, how a Rose e'er blooming
From tender stem hath sprung!
Of Jesse's lineage coming
As men of old have sung.
It came a flow'ret bright,
Amid the cold of winter,
When half spent was the night.

Isaiah 'twas foretold it,
The Rose I have in mind,
With Mary we behold it,
The Virgin Mother kind.
To show God's love aright
She bore to us a Savior,
When half spent was the night.

The Rosebud

Queen of fragrance, lovely rose,
The beauties of thy leaves disclose!
The winter's past, the tempests fly,
Soft gales breathe gently through the sky:
The lark sweet warbling on the wing
Salutes the gay return of spring:
The silver dews, the vernal showers,
Call forth a bloomy waste of flowers;
The joyous fields, the shady woods,
Are clothed with green, or swell with buds;
Then haste thy beauties to disclose,
Queen of fragrance, lovely rose!

—WILLIAM BROOME

The Nightingale and The Rose

by Oscar Wilde

"She said that she would dance with me if I brought her red roses," cried the young Student, "but in all my garden there is no red rose." From her nest in the holm-oak tree the Nightingale heard him, and she looked out through the leaves and wondered.

"No red rose in all my garden!" he cried, and his beautiful eyes filled with tears. "Ah, on what little things does happiness depend! I have read all that the wise men have written, and all the secrets of philosophy are mine, yet for want of a red rose is my life made wretched."

"Here at last is a true lover," said the Nightingale. "Night after night have I sung of him, though I knew him not: night after night have I told his story to the stars, and now I see him. His hair is dark as the hyacinth-blossom, and his lips are red as the rose of his desire; but passion has made his face like pale ivory, and sorrow has set her seal upon his brow."

"The Prince gives a ball to-morrow night," murmured the young Student, "and my love will be of the company. If I bring her a red rose she will dance with me till dawn. If I bring her a red rose, I shall hold her in my arms, and she will lean her head upon my shoulder, and her hand will be clasped in mine. But there is no red rose in my garden, so I

The Nightingale and the Rose

shall sit lonely, and she will pass me by. She will have no heed of me, and my heart will break."

"Here indeed is the true lover," said the Nightingale. "What I sing of, he suffers: what is joy to me, to him is pain. Surely Love is a wonderful thing. It is more precious than emeralds, and dearer than fine opals. Pearls and pomegranates cannot buy it, nor is it set forth in the market-place. It may not be purchased of the merchants, nor can it be weighed out in the balance for gold."

"The musicians will sit in their gallery," said the young Student, "and play upon their stringed instruments, and my love will dance to the sound of the harp and the violin. She will dance so lightly that her feet will not touch the floor, and the courtiers in their gay dresses will throng round her. But with me she will not dance, for I have no red rose to give her;" and he flung himself down on the grass, and buried his face in his hands, and wept.

"Why is he weeping?" asked a little Green Lizard, as he ran past him with his tail in the air.

"Why, indeed?" said a Butterfly, who was fluttering about after a sunbeam.

"Why, indeed?" whispered a Daisy to his neighbor, in a soft, low voice.

"He is weeping for a red rose," said the Nightingale.

The Nightingale and the Rose

"For a red rose?" they cried; "how very ridiculous!" and the little Lizard, who was something of a cynic, laughed outright.

But the Nightingale understood the secret of the Student's sorrow, and she sat silent in the oak-tree, and thought about the mystery of Love.

Suddenly she spread her brown wings for flight, and soared into the air. She passed through the grove like a shadow, and like a shadow she sailed across the garden.

In the centre of the grass-plot was standing a beautiful Rose-tree, and when she saw it she flew over to it, and lit upon a spray.

"Give me a red rose," she cried, "and I will sing you my sweetest song." But the Tree shook its head.

"My roses are white," it answered; "as white as the foam of the sea, and whiter than the snow upon the mountain. But go to my brother who grows round the old sun-dial, and perhaps he will give you what you want."

So the Nightingale flew over to the Rose-tree that was growing round the old sun-dial.

"Give me a red rose," she cried, "and I will sing you my sweetest song." But the Tree shook its head.

"My roses are yellow," is answered; "as yellow as the hair of the mermaiden who sits upon an amber throne, and yellower than the daffodil that blooms in the meadow before the mower comes with his scythe. But go to my brother who grows beneath the Student's window, and perhaps he will give you what you want."

The Nightingale and the Rose

So the Nightingale flew over to the Rose-tree that was growing beneath the Student's window.

"Give me a red rose," she cried, "and I will sing you my sweetest song." But the Tree shook its head.

"My roses are red," it answered, "as red as the feet of the dove, and redder than the great fans of coral that wave and wave in the ocean-cavern. But the winter has chilled my veins, and the frost has nipped my buds, and the storm has broken my branches, and I shall have no roses at all this year."

"One red rose is all I want," cried the Nightingale, "only one red rose! Is there no way by which I can get it?"

"There is a way," answered the Tree; "but it is so terrible that I dare not tell it to you."

"Tell it to me," said the Nightingale, "I am not afraid."

"If you want a red rose," said the Tree, "you must build it out of music by moonlight, and stain it with your own heart's-blood. You must sing to me with your breast against a thorn. All night long you must sing to me, and the thorn must pierce your heart, and your life-blood must flow into my veins, and become mine."

"Death is a great price to pay for a red rose," cried the Nightingale, "and Life is very dear to all. It is pleasant to sit in the green wood, and to watch the Sun in his chariot of gold, and the Moon in her chariot of pearl. Sweet is the scent of the hawthorn, and sweet are the bluebells

The Nightingale and the Rose

that hide in the valley, and the heather that blows on the hill.

Yet Love is better than Life, and what is the heart of a bird compared to the heart of a man?"

So she spread her brown wings for flight, and soared into the air. She swept over the garden like a shadow, and like a shadow she sailed through the grove.

The young Student was still lying on the grass, where she had left him, and the tears were not yet dry in his beautiful eyes.

"Be happy," cried the Nightingale, "be happy; you shall have your red rose. I will build it out of music by moonlight, and stain it with my own heart's-blood. All that I ask of you in return is that you will be a true lover, for Love is wiser than Philosophy, though he is wise, and mightier than Power, though he is mighty. Flame-colored are his wings, and colored like flame is his body. His lips are sweet as honey, and his breath is like frankincense."

The Student looked up from the grass, and listened, but he could not understand what the Nightingale was saying to him, for he only knew the things that are written down in books.

But the Oak-tree understood, and felt sad, for he was very fond of the little Nightingale, who had built her nest in his branches.

"Sing me one last song," he whispered;

The Nightingale and the Rose

"I shall feel lonely when you are gone."

So the Nightingale sang to the Oak-tree, and her voice was like water bubbling from a silver jar.

When she had finished her song, the Student got up, and pulled a note-book and a lead-pencil out of his pocket.

"She has form," he said to himself, as he walked away through the grove—"that cannot be denied to her; but has she got feeling? I am afraid not. In fact, she is like most artists; she is all style without any sincerity. She would not sacrifice herself for others. She thinks merely of music, and everybody knows that the arts are selfish. Still, it must be admitted that she has some beautiful notes in her voice. What a pity it is that they do not mean anything, or do any practical good!" And he went into his room, and lay down on his little pallet-bed, and began to think of his love; and, after a time, he fell asleep.

And when the moon shone in the heavens the Nightingale flew to the Rose-tree, and set her breast against the thorn. All night long she sang, with her breast against the thorn, and the cold crystal Moon leaned down and listened. All night long she sang, and the thorn went deeper and deeper into her breast, and her life-blood ebbed away from her.

She sang first of the birth of love in the heart of a boy and a girl. And on the topmost spray of the Rose-tree there blossomed a marvellous rose, petal following petal, as song followed song. Pale was it, at first, as the mist that hangs over the river—pale as the feet of the morning, and silver

The Nightingale and the Rose

as the wings of the dawn. As the shadow of a rose in a mirror of
silver, as the shadow of a rose in a water-pool, so was the rose
that blossomed on the topmost spray of the Tree.

But the Tree cried to the Nightingale to press closer against the thorn.
"Press closer, little Nightingale," cried the Tree, "or the Day will come
before the rose is finished."

So the Nightingale pressed closer against the thorn, and louder and
louder grew her song, for she sang of the birth of passion in the soul of a
man and a maid.

And a delicate flush of pink came into the leaves of the rose, like the
flush in the face of the bridegroom when he kisses the lips of the bride. But
the thorn had not yet reached her heart, so the rose's heart remained white,
for only a Nightingale's heart's-blood can crimson the heart of a rose.

And the Tree cried to the Nightingale to press closer against the thorn.
"Press closer, little Nightingale," cried the Tree, "or the Day will come
before the rose if finished."

So the Nightingale pressed closer against the thorn, and the thorn
touched her heart, and a fierce pang of pain shot through her. Bitter, bitter
was the pain, and wilder and wilder grew her song, for she sang of the
Love that is perfected by Death, of the Love that dies not in the tomb.

And the marvellous rose became crimson, like the rose of the eastern
sky. Crimson was the girdle of petals, and crimson as a ruby was the heart.

But the Nightingale's voice grew fainter, and her little wings began to

The Nightingale and the Rose

beat, and a film came over her eyes. Fainter and fainter grew her song, and she felt something choking her in her throat.

Then she gave one last burst of music. The white Moon heard it, and she forgot the dawn, and lingered on in the sky. The red rose heard it, and it trembled all over with ecstasy, and opened its petals to the cold morning air. Echo bore it to her purple cavern in the hills, and woke the sleeping shepherds from their dreams. It floated through the reeds of the river, and they carried its message to the sea.

"Look, look!" cried the Tree, "the rose is finished now;" but the Nightingale made no answer, for she was lying dead in the long grass, with the thorn in her heart.

And at noon the Student opened his window and looked out.

"Why, what a wonderful piece of luck!" he cried; "here is a red rose! I have never seen any rose like it in all my life. It is so beautiful that I am sure it has a long Latin name;" and he leaned down and plucked it.

Then he put on his hat, and ran up to the Professor's house with the rose in his hand.

The daughter of the Professor was sitting in the doorway winding blue silk on a reel, and her little dog was lying at her feet.

"You said that you would dance with me if I brought you a red rose," cried the Student. "Here is the reddest rose in all the world. You will wear it tonight next your heart, and as we dance together it will tell you how I love you."

The Nightingale and the Rose

But the girl frowned.

"I am afraid it will not go with my dress," she answered; "and, besides, the Chamberlain's nephew has sent me some real jewels, and everybody knows that jewels cost far more than flowers."

"Well, upon my word, you are very ungrateful," said the Student angrily; and he threw the rose into the street, where it fell into the gutter, and a cartwheel went over it.

"Ungrateful!" said the girl. "I tell you what, you are very rude; and, after all, who are you? Only a Student. Why, I don't believe you have even got silver buckles to your shoes as the Chamberlain's nephew has;" and she got up from her chair and went into the house.

"What a silly thing Love is!" said the Student as he walked away. "It is not half as useful as Logic, for it does not prove anything, and it is always telling one of things that are not going to happen, and making one believe things that are not true. In fact, it is quite unpractical, and, and in this age to be practical is everything, I shall go back to Philosophy and study Metaphysics."

So he returned to his room and pulled out a great dusty book, and began to read.

Nobody Knows This Little Rose

Nobody knows this little Rose—
It might a pilgrim be
Did I not take it from the ways
And lift it up to thee.
Only a Bee will miss it—
Only a Butterfly,
Hastening from far journey—
On its breast to lie—
Only a Bird will wonder—
Only a Breeze will sigh—
Ah Little Rose—how easy
For such as thee to die!

—EMILY DICKINSON

The wilderness and the solitary place shall be glad for them: and the desert shall rejoice, and blossom as the rose.

—Isaiah 35:1

Rose Hips Tea

1 CUP HIGH-QUALITY BLACK TEA LEAVES
$3/4$ OZ CHOPPED ROSE HIPS
$1/2$ CUP DRIED ORGANIC ROSE PETALS
2 TABLESPOONS DRIED JASMINE FLOWERS
1 TABLESPOON DRIED ORANGE PEEL, FRESHLY GRATED
3 STICKS CINNAMON, CRUMBLED
1 TABLESPOON GROUND NUTMEG
2 TEASPOONS CLOVES, CRUSHED

Mix all ingredients in a mixing bowl. Store in an airtight container. Use one teaspoon or more per cup of boiling water, to brew to your desired strength.

Rose Fragrances

When you think of the scent of a rose, what comes to mind? Most people probably think of the smell of the Damask rose, that signature combination of floral, sweet, and spicy scents that is commonly associated with the blooms. But roses have so many other fragrances to explore! While discerning the specific scents of these flowers can be somewhat subjective, many roses have distinct fruit, spice, herbal, or floral aromas. Create a rose garden that smells like fruit basket or choose pepper and clove-smelling plants for a spicier scent. Check out these suggested varieties to create a garden with its own signature perfume.

Rose Fragrances

Classes of Scents and Roses

APPLE
Rosa eglanteria

DAMASK
Damask and Portland roses

FLORAL
Species roses

PINE, CITRUS, HERBAL
Moss roses

MIXED FRUIT
Chinas and Hybrid Musk

MUSK
Noisettes and Hybrid Musk

SPICE
Rosa rugosa, Floribundas, and Chinas

TEA
Teas and Noisettes

Specific Scents and Varieties

ALMOND
Roseraie de la Hay, Mary Rose

APPLE
Apple Jack, New Dawn, Coral Dawn, *Rosa winchuriana* hybrids, Lady Penzance, Debutante, Bonica

BANANA
Rosa mulligani

CINNAMON TOAST
Sunsprite

Rose Fragrances

CLOVE
Rosa rugosa, America, Wild Spice, Hansa

HONEY
Gourmet Popcorn, Golden CelebrationHoneysweet,

LEMON
Mme. Hardy, Sutter's Gold, White Lightnin', Lemon Zest

LICORICE
Austrian Copper, Teasing Georgia Snowbird, *Rosa foetida*, Persian Yellow

MUSK
Himalayan Musk Rose, *Rosa moschata*

ORANGE
Woburn Abbey

PEPPER
Old Blush, Maggie

PINEAPPLE
Rosa multiflora

RASPBERRY
Mme. Isaac Perreire, Ceriese Bouquet, Zephirine Drouhin

SPICE
Jens Munk, Magic Carpet, *Rosa cinnamonea*, Double Delight

STRAWBERRY
Chrysler Imperial, Marechal Niel

TEA
Duke of York, Gloire de Dijon , Graham Thomas, Queen Elizabeth

I was a child. I remember
gathering wild roses.
They had so many thorns—
I didn't want to break them—
I believed they were buds
and were going to flower.

Then I met you. O love,
you had so many thorns!
I didn't want to strip them—
I believed they would flower.

All this I review today
and smile—smile
and wander the roads
driven by the wind.
I was a child.

—LUCIAN BLAGA

The Gardener's July

by Karel Čapek

In July, according to the immutable law of gardeners, roses are grafted. It is usually done like this: a briar, a wilding, or stock on which the grafting should be done, is got ready, and then a great amount of bast, and finally a gardening or grafting-knife. When all is ready the gardener tries the blade of the knife on the tip of his thumb; if the grafting-knife is sufficiently sharp it gashes his thumb and leaves an open and bleeding wound. This is wrapped in several yards of lint, from which a bud, rather full and big, develops on the finger. This is called grafting a rose. If a briar is not at hand it is possible to achieve the same result on another occasion, as when making cuttings, pruning side branches or dead flowers, or trimming bushes and suchlike.

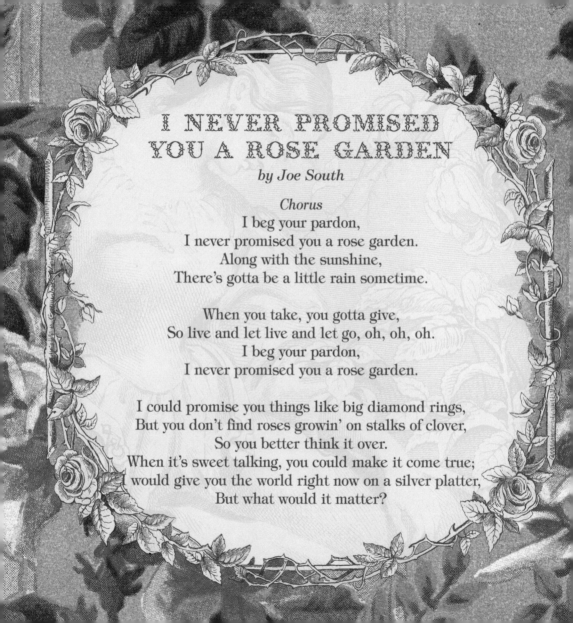

I NEVER PROMISED
YOU A ROSE GARDEN

by Joe South

Chorus
I beg your pardon,
I never promised you a rose garden.
Along with the sunshine,
There's gotta be a little rain sometime.

When you take, you gotta give,
So live and let live and let go, oh, oh, oh.
I beg your pardon,
I never promised you a rose garden.

I could promise you things like big diamond rings,
But you don't find roses growin' on stalks of clover,
So you better think it over.
When it's sweet talking, you could make it come true;
I would give you the world right now on a silver platter,
But what would it matter?

So smile for a while and let's be jolly;
Love shouldn't be so melancholy.
Come along and share the good times while we can.

Chorus

I could sing you a tune and promise you the moon,
But if that's what it takes to hold you,
I'd just as soon let you go,
But there's one thing I want you to know.
You better look before you leap, still waters run deep,
And there won't always be someone there, to pull you out.
And you know what I'm talkin' about.
So smile for a while and let's be jolly;
Love shouldn't be so melancholy
Come along and share the good times while we can.

Chorus

Feeding and Watering Roses

Many people believe that roses require more maintenance than other plants, but the truth is that most roses need only a sunny spot, occasional watering, and a bit of fertilizer now and again. These tips provide easy ways to water and feed your garden and will keep your roses growing beautifully.

WATERING

SOAK: Soak the roots of your roses rather than setting a sprinkler on them from above. When the buds and foliage of the roses get too wet, you open the door for fungi, like black spot or rust.

WATER IN THE MORNING. This allows the whole day for the plant leaves to dry off should any water splash onto them.

WATER SLOWLY: Using a watering can or hose, pour the water slowly around the base of the rose and allow it to sink in before adding more. This will prevent splashing that can spread disease and fungus.

Feeding and Watering Roses

WATER DEEPLY: This encourages the roots to grow more deeply. With deep roots, your plant will be able to reach ground water when the weather is dry. Roses need about an inch of water a week, so if your garden is going through a dry period, be sure to give your roses a good soaking once or twice a week.

❧

PAY ATTENTION TO YOUR PLANT: There are times when your roses will need more water than others. When they are in full bloom, exposed to strong winds, or the temperature rises above 80°F, they will need a good soaking to stay hydrated. Also, roses that have just been planted, those planted in containers, sandy soil, or on a slope will need extra water.

FEEDING

FERTILIZE IN SPRING AND EARLY SUMMER: Fertilizer boosts your roses' ability to produce new shoots, which is exactly what you want at the beginning of the growing season. Roses need to toughen up their canes and foliage at the end of the season to survive the winter, so give your last treatment in late summer and hold off on fertilizing in the fall.

❧

Feeding and Watering Roses

DON'T FERTILIZE NEWLY PLANTED ROSES: Fertilizing encourages top growth, and when you first plant your roses, you want them to develop a strong, healthy root network first. Wait about a year after planting before fertilizing your roses.

❧

KNOW YOUR FERTILIZER'S TIMETABLE: Organic fertilizers break down over time as microbes digest them, therefore the nutrients they provide to the soil aren't always immediately available. These fertilizers enrich the soil gradually but consistently over the years. Inorganic fertilizers are water-soluble so the vitamins reach the rose roots right away. These are great to give your plant if it is in urgent need of nutrients, but they do not linger in the soil as long.

❧

CHECK THE NUTRIENTS IN YOUR SOIL: You can take a sample of your soil to a lab to get it professionally analyzed or buy a soil testing kit to

Feeding and Watering Roses

determine the pH and levels of nutrients in your garden (check with your local nursery for suggestions on labs or testing kits). Roses do best in neutral to slightly acidic soil conditions (pH of 6.5 to 7.0). If needed, you can acidify the soil by adding organic matter, or make the soil more alkaline by adding lime.

❧

SUPPLY THE MISSING MINERALS: The three most important compounds for your roses are nitrogen, phosphorus, and potassium. Once you have tested your soil, you will know which ones to supplement. Fish meal is a great source for all three nutrients; alfalfa meal will boost nitrogen, bonemeal will increase the soil's phosphorus, and kelp extract will raise the potassium level. Ask for advice at your local nursery on how much of each additive to use in your garden to perfect the soil.

❧

World Famous
Gardens

A ll around the world horticultural societies, municipalities, and philanthropists have created rose gardens and opened them for public view. Here is a list of a few favorite gardens of rose lovers everywhere.

THE GARDENS OF THE AMERICAN ROSE SOCIETY, SHREVEPORT, LOUISIANA

This is the largest park devoted to roses in the United States. It has fountains and winding paths lined with literally thousands of roses.

THE ROSE GARDEN AT THE MONTREAL BOTANICAL GARDEN, MONTREAL, CANADA

Remarkably, 10,000 roses—including a fine collection of Old Garden Roses and modern shrub roses—grow in the cold

northern climate of Montreal. This garden is also an educational center for the winter care of roses.

CITY OF PORTLAND, PORTLAND, OREGON

Oregon Portland Parks and Recreation District and the American Rose Society curate three rose gardens in this "City of Roses." Peninsula Park, near the center of the city, is a sunken garden of modern design with more than 8,800 fragrant roses. The International Rose Test Garden is Portland's most notable landmark with spectacular views and a garden of more than 8,000 roses. Ladd's Addition Rose Garden, the smallest and most intimate of the three, boasts 3,200 roses popular in the early 20th century.

ROSARIUM IN THE ARBORETUM IN THE FORESTRY SCHOOL, ZVOLEN, CZECH REPUBLIC

This six-acre garden with over 14,000 roses of 1,000 different varieties displays a fine collection of older rose varieties from Yalta, Budapest, and Moscow.

SAINT ANNE'S PARK, DUBLIN, IRELAND

This park, formerly part of the Guinness Estate, was created

over 100 years ago. The Rose Garden was added in the early 1970s by The Royal Horticultural Society and the Dublin Corporation Parks Department. It covers ten acres of the park with thousands of flowers.

La Roseraie de l'Hay du Val de Marne, France

This 27-acre garden is the oldest devoted exclusively to roses. The collection of 25,000 roses in 6,000 varieties includes Old Roses grown in the early days of French hybridization, as well as 40 special varieties known as "Roses of Malmaison" from the time of the Empress Josephine.

TeAwamutu, New Zealand (South of Cambridge)

A former military constabulary, TeAwamutu, nicknamed "Rosetown," has more than a dozen notable rose gardens, including the formal rose garden on Gorst Avenue which showcases 2,500 rose bushes.

Kew Gardens, London, Great Britain

Although this collection contains only 550 roses, the varieties are exceptional. There are climbers, a hedge of the famous hybrid

musk rose "Penelope," and—most interestingly—a healthy "Mme. Caroline Testout" that is nearly 100 years old.

QUEEN MARY'S GARDEN, REGENT'S PARK, LONDON, GREAT BRITAIN

This is England's National Rose Garden—and one of the most celebrated rose gardens in the world. It contains 40,000 roses of every kind planted in single-variety and mixed-variety beds.

PARC DE LA TETE D'OR LYON, FRANCE

This park is comprised of three rose gardens which cover more than 17 acres with an astounding 100,000 roses: the Rosarium is exclusively devoted to rose trials for French roses; La Roseraie Paysagere Nouvelle, with 3,000 rose bushes and 350 varieties, is esteemed to be the most beautiful rose garden in France; and the Lyon Botanical Garden is committed to chronicling the history of the rose.

ROSETO DI ROMA, MONTE AVENTINO, ROME, ITALY

The city rose garden looks like an amphitheater—it is planted in a semi-circle with over 5,000 plants in 1,000 different varieties. There are climbing roses as well as species roses in the collection.

World Famous Gardens

ROSARIUM SANGERHAUSEN, SANGERHAUSEN, GERMANY

Known as "the living history of the rose," this collection rivals
La Roseraie de l'Hay du Val de Marne as the finest European
rose collection with its more than 50,000 roses of 6,000 varieties
representing every class of roses.

THE ROSARIUM OF THE GERMAN ROSE SOCIETY, CITY OF DORMAND, GERMANY

This rose garden hosts over two million visitors a year. The
40,000 plants of 2,500 varieties are arranged according to their
country of origin, which has its own hybridizers grouped together.

ROSALEDA DEL PARQUE DEL OESTE, MADRID, SPAIN

The City of Madrid maintains this 22-acre garden with 300 beds
of 100 plants each. The Rosaleda is reputed to have the largest
and finest rose blooms anywhere in the world.

THE BERKELEY ROSE GARDEN, BERKELEY, CALIFORNIA

This garden in the Berkeley hills is a terraced amphitheater with
3,000 rose bushes and 250 varieties. It has a breathtaking view of
the sunset behind the Golden Gate Bridge from a redwood pergola.

To Helen

There fell a silvery-silken veil of light,
With quietude, and sultriness, and slumber,
Upon the upturned faces of a thousand
Roses that grew in an enchanted garden,
Where no wind dared to stir, unless on tiptoe—
Fell on the upturn'd faces of these roses
That gave out, in return for the love-light,
Their odorous souls in an ecstatic death—
Fell on the upturn'd faces of these roses
That smiled and died in this parterre, enchanted.
By thee, and by the poetry of thy presence.

—EDGAR ALLAN POE

In the garden mystery glows

The secret is hidden in the rose.

—Farid ud-Din Attar

Alice's Adventures in Wonderland

Lewis Carroll

A large rose-tree stood near the entrance of the garden: the roses growing on it were white, but there were three gardeners at it, busily painting them red. Alice thought this a very curious thing, and she went nearer to watch them . . .

"Would you tell me, please," said Alice, a little timidly, "why are you painting those roses?"

Five and Seven said nothing, but looked at Two. Two began, in a low voice, "Why, the fact is, you see, Miss, this here ought to have been a red rose-tree, and we put a white one in by mistake; and, if the Queen was to find it out, we should all have our heads cut off, you know. So you see, Miss, we're doing our best, afore she comes, to—" At this moment, Five, who had been anxiously looking across the garden, called out "The Queen! The Queen!" and the three gardeners instantly threw themselves flat on their faces. . .

When the procession came opposite to Alice, they all stopped and looked at her, and the Queen said, severely, "Who is this?" She said it to the Knave of Hearts, who only bowed and smiled in reply.

"Idiot!" said the Queen, tossing her head impatiently; and, turning to Alice, she went on: "What's your name, child?"

"My name is Alice, so please your majesty," said Alice very politely;

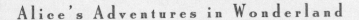

but she added, to herself, "Why they're only a pack of cards, after all. I needn't be afraid of them!"

"And who are *these?*" said the Queen, pointing to the three gardeners who were lying round the rose-tree; for, you see, as they were lying on their faces, and the pattern on their backs was the same as the rest of the pack, she could not tell whether they were gardeners, or soldiers, or three of her own children . . .

"Get up!" said the Queen in a shrill, loud voice, and the three gardeners instantly jumped up, and began bowing to the King, the Queen, the royal children, and everybody else.

"Leave off that!" screamed the Queen. "You make me giddy." And then, turning to the rose-tree, she went on, "What have you been doing here?"

"May it please your Majesty," said Two, in a very humble tone, going down on one knee as he spoke, "we were trying—"

"*I* see!" said the Queen, who had meanwhile been examining the roses. "Off with their heads!" and the procession moved on, three of the soldiers remaining behind to execute the unfortunate gardeners, who ran to Alice for protection.

"You sha'n't be beheaded!" said Alice, and she put them into a large flower-pot that stood near. The three soldiers wandered about for a minute or two, looking for them, and then quietly marched off after the others.

"Are their heads off?" shouted the Queen.

"Their heads are gone, if it please your Majesty!" the soldiers shouted in reply.

Rose Cake

2¹/₄ CUP SIFTED ALL-PURPOSE FLOUR

1¹/₂ CUP SUGAR

2 TEASPOONS BAKING POWDER

¹/₂ TEASPOON BAKING SODA

¹/₂ TEASPOON SALT

¹/₂ CUP COOKING OIL

³/₄ CUP WATER

3 TO 4 TEASPOONS ROSE WATER

1 TEASPOON VANILLA

5 EGGS, SEPARATED

¹/₂ TEASPOON CREAM OF TARTAR

1 CUP ORGANIC ROSE PETALS, CLEANED
   AND ROUGHLY CHOPPED

GLAZE:

1 CUP POWDERED SUGAR

2–4 TABLESPOONS HEAVY CREAM

¹/₂ TEASPOON ROSE WATER (SEE P. 68)

1 OR 2 DROPS RED FOOD COLORING
   (OPTIONAL)

ADDITIONAL ORGANIC ROSE PETALS
   FOR GARNISH (OPTIONAL)

1. Preheat oven at 350°F.
2. Sift the flour, sugar, baking powder, baking soda, and salt together into a very large mixing bowl.
3. Add the oil, water, rose water,

vanilla, and egg yolks, and beat until smooth.

4. Beat the egg whites with cream of tartar in a large bowl until very stiff peaks form.

5. Add one third of the batter to your egg whites, and fold in with a large, wooden spoon. You are working to incorporate as much air as possible to provide lightness to your cake.

6. Continue adding batter to egg whites, folding just until incorporated. Fold in rose petals.

7. Pour the batter into a greased 10-inch tube pan.

8. Bake for 1 hour or until a cake tester comes out clean.

9. Invert pan onto a plate to cool.

10. Prepare the glaze while the cake cools.

11. Combine powdered sugar, cream, and rose water, beating until smooth.

12. If you'd like, add food coloring for a more appealing shade of "rose."

13. Slowly pour the glaze over the cooled cake, letting it run down the sides.

14. Garnish with additional rose petals and serve.

Serves 10

Little Known Rose Facts

According to ancient mythology, roses had no thorns until Cupid kissed a flower and was stung by a bee. He was so angry that he shot his arrows into the rose bed, giving the plants their thorns.

The aphrodisiac quality of roses has long been documented. Allegedly, Cleopatra even laid a carpet of rose petals in her palace to aid in her seduction of Marc Antony.

According to legend, rose oil was discovered at the wedding of a Mogul princess. Rosewater filled a canal that ran through a garden, and in the heat, the essential rose oil from the fallen petals separated and floated to the top of the water.

Little Known Rose Facts

The world's largest rosebush can be found in Tombstone, Arizona. This one-hundred-year-old bush produces more than 200,000 flowers in full bloom, and its trunk measures almost six feet around.

Rose oil and rosewater have mild antiseptic and healing properties, and can aid dry and sensitive skin.

Aphrodite, the Greek goddess of love, was born on the island of Cyprus from sea foam blown by the west wind. White roses grew from the place where the foam fell on the land and red roses sprung from the place where Aphrodite's blood fell when she scratched herself on the thorns of the white roses.

If You Love Roses

If you love the roses—so do I. I wish
The sky would rain down roses,
    as they rain
From off the shaken bush.
    Why will it not?
Then all the valley would be pink
    and white
And soft to tread on. They would
    fall as light
As feathers, smelling sweet; and
    it would be
Like sleeping and like waking,
    all at once!

—GEORGE ELIOT

Roses, Roses, Roses

by S. Reynolds Hole

Enter, then, the rose garden when the first sunshine sparkles in the dew, and enjoy with thankful happiness one of the loveliest scenes of earth. What a diversity, and yet what a harmony, of colour! There are white roses, striped roses, blush roses, pink roses, rose roses, carmine roses, crimson roses, scarlet roses, vermilion roses, maroon roses, purple roses, roses almost black, and roses of a glowing gold. What a diversity, and yet what a harmony outline! Dwarf roses and climbing roses, roses closely carpeting the ground, roses that droop in snowy foam like fountains, and roses that stretch out their branches upwards as though they would kiss the sun; roses 'in shape no bigger than an agate-stone on the fore-finger of an alderman', and roses five inches across; roses in clusters, and roses blooming singly; roses in bud, in their glory, decline, and fall . . . He is no true florist who has never felt the springs of his heart troubled, surging, overflowing, as he looked on such a scene of beauty as that which I so feebly describe. Such visions seem at first too bright, too dazzling, for our weakly sight: we are awed, and we shrink to feel ourselves in a Divine presence; the spirit is oppressed by a happiness which it is unworthy, unable to apprehend, and it finds relief in tears.

Fighting Bugs and Disease

Choosing the right roses is the first step to growing healthy, vigorous plants, and keeping your garden free of pests and disease. If you want to avoid using pesticides, choose rose varieties that are hardy and disease resistant. Provide the right start for your plants by enhancing the soil with organic materials suited to the variety you chose. Water carefully by moistening the roots, and avoid drenching the foliage as this will lead to mildew. Lastly, prune your rosebushes to remove any hint of disease and to encourage air circulation. Even with all your best efforts, your roses may develop fungus and mildew. These tips will help you identify the source of your problems and offer advice on keeping your roses healthy and beautiful.

Most Common Diseases

Black Spot: Small, circular black spots with yellow edges form on the leaves. If left unchecked, leaves will turn yellow and fall from the plant. Black spot is most common in humid and wet conditions. To prevent spreading, remove any leaves tainted with black spot, and prune back infected canes. Apply antitranspirants and sulfur

Fighting Bugs and Disease

treatments and consult your local nursery about the appropriate amounts and intervals for your rose type. Be sure to rake up any dead leaves, and burn or dispose of carefully; do not compost.

❧

Downy Mildew: A fungus that thrives in cool, damp climates, downy mildew shows up as purple spots on the leaves and infected canes. Foliage will turn yellow and fall off and infected canes can die off over the winter if not pruned. Remove and destroy all infected leaves and canes (do not compost) and apply antitranspirants.

❧

Powdery Mildew: If new leaves on your rose curl up and become covered with a white dusty substance, most likely it is powdery mildew. This fungus often appears after drought and on shrubs in shady areas with poor air circulation. Apply antitranspirants and give weekly sulfur treatments, and remove all infected leaves and canes.

❧

Rust: Bright orange pustules on the backside of your rose leaves indicate a case of rust. Warm, wet

Fighting Bugs and Disease

conditions encourage the growth of this fungus, which is more common in southern and northwestern areas of North America. Prune off affected leaves and canes and spray with baking soda and horticultural oil on a weekly basis.

❧

Canker: If you see brown or reddish sunken spots on the canes of your roses, your plants could have canker. This bacterial infection invades through cuts or wounds on the canes and often shows up when the plants come out of dormancy in the spring. Prune off the affected part of the cane; cut at a 45-degree angle just above a node.

❧

Crown Gall: Caused by bacteria that live in the soil, crown gall produces round growths about 2 inches in diameter at the base of the plant that start out green and turn brown and woody with age. It rarely affects roses that are planted deep enough in the ground, but once contracted, it is difficult to control. Try paring off the damaged area with a sharp knife (making sure to disinfect it after use). If that doesn't work, destroy the shrub and do not plant roses in the same spot.

❧

Fighting Bugs and Disease

Rose Mosaic: This is a viral infection that cannot be treated, but can be avoided by purchasing certified virus-free stock. Mosaic is spread through grafting, but there is little natural spreading of the disease. Roses with mosaic exhibit leaves with yellow or lime green color in blotches, wavy lines, or an oak-leaf pattern. Plants with mosaic do not need to be replaced as long as they grow in an acceptable manner.

⁊

Rosette: This deadly viral infection also is not treatable, and you should destroy any rose that contracts it. The symptoms are thick burgundy or lime green bristly growth resembling a witch's broom, with rubbery thorns and aberrant leaf shape. Also, destroy any Rosa mulitflora plants that reside on your property if your roses come down with rosette, as these plants harbor the mites that transmit the disease.

Bugs and Other Pests

Aphids: These tiny translucent insects suck the juice from rose leaves and secret a sticky substance that attracts ants and black spot

Fighting Bugs and Disease

fungus. They cause the leaves to curl and buds to wither and die. Spray leaves with a steady stream of water to remove the bugs, or try an insecticidal soap.

Leaf-cutter Bees: Circle or C-shaped cutouts on your rose leaves indicate leaf-cutter bees. They use the leaf material to build their nests and do not do any permanent damage to the plants.

Spider Mites: Leaves take on a bronze sheen and become dry when infested with spider mites. Spray with a steady stream of water to rid the plant of adult mites and treat with insecticidal soap three times (leave a day or two between treatments to kill any further generations).

Cane Borers: These are the larvae of beetles that burrow down into the canes, hollowing them out. Canes above the borer quickly wilt and die. To treat, prune canes back to well below tunneled-out area.

Fighting Bugs and Disease

Scale: Crusty shelled bugs attach themselves to foliage stems and canes, causing stunted growth, wilted leaves, and defoliation. Prune out heavily infested canes and treat plants with horticultural oil in the spring to prevent reinfestation.

❦

By taking preventive measures, you can eliminate many of these common problems. Prune back leaves and canes at the first signs of disease, seal the refuse in a plastic bag and dispose of it. Rake up any fallen leaves regularly and remove mulch at the end of the season as both can harbor fungus and mildew spores. Strip off any remaining foliage at the end of the growing season and throw away; do not compost. Also, always be sure to sanitize your pruning shears with alcohol or a mild bleach solution to prevent the spread of infection. Water your roses from the roots and not from overhead, as wet leaves encourage mold growth. Plant your roses in areas with good air circulation, and prune the plants to let the breezes blow through them. Ask your nursery for advice on other organic or chemical foods and treatments for your specific rose types.

❦

The Snail and the Rosebush

by Hans Christian Andersen

In the centre of the garden stood a Rosebush in full bloom. Under it lay a Snail, who had a great deal in him, according to himself. "Wait till my time comes," said he; "I shall do a great deal more than yield roses . . ."

"I expect an immense deal from you," said the Rosebush. "May I ask when it is to come forth?"

"I shall take my time," replied the Snail. "You are always in such a hurry with your work, that curiosity about it is never excited."

The following year the Snail lay in the sunshine under the Rosebush; it was already in bud and the buds had begun to expand into full-blown flowers, always fresh, always new. And the Snail crept half out, stretched forth its feelers, and then drew them in again. "Everything looks just the same as last year, there is no progress to be seen anywhere. The Rosebush is covered with roses—it will never get beyond that."

The summer passed, the autumn passed; the Rosebush had yielded roses and buds up to the time that the snow fell. The Rosebush bowed down towards the ground, the Snail crept into the earth.

A new year commenced, the Rosebush revived, and the Snail came forth again. "You are now only an old stick of a rose-bush," said he; "you must expect to wither away soon. You have given the world all that was in you . . . Have you not occasionally reflected why you blossomed, and in what way

The Snail and the Rosebush

you blossomed—how in one way and not in another?"

"No," answered the Rosebush; "I blossomed in gladness for I could not do otherwise . . . I was obliged to blossom. It was my life; I could not do otherwise."

"You have had a very easy life," remarked the Snail.

"To be sure, much has been granted to me," said the Rosebush, "but no more will be bestowed on me now . . . Yes! I have only been able to give roses; but you—you who have got so much—what have you given to the world? What will you give it?"

"What have I given? What will I give? I spit upon it! It is good for nothing! I have no interest in it. Produce your roses—you cannot do more than that . . . I am going into myself, and shall remain there. The world is nothing to me."

And so the Snail withdrew into his house, and closed it up.

"What a sad pity it is!" exclaimed the Rosebush. "I cannot creep into shelter however much I might wish it. I must always spring out, spring out into roses. The leaves fall off and they fly away in the wind. But I saw one of the roses laid in a psalm book belonging to the mistress of the house; another of my roses was placed on the breast of a young and beautiful girl, and another was kissed by a child's soft lips in an ecstasy of joy. I was so charmed at all this: it was a real happiness to me—one of the pleasant remembrances of my life."

And the rose bloomed on in innocence, while the Snail retired into his slimy house—the world was nothing to him!

The Rose

And I think of roses, roses,
White and red, in the wide six-hundred-
   foot greenhouses,
And my father standing astride the
   cement benches,
Lifting me high over the four-foot stems,
   the Mrs. Russells,
      and his own elaborate hybrids,
And how those flowerheads seemed
   to flow toward me, to beckon
      me, only a child, out of myself.

What need for heaven, then,
With that man, and those roses?

           —THEODORE ROETHKE

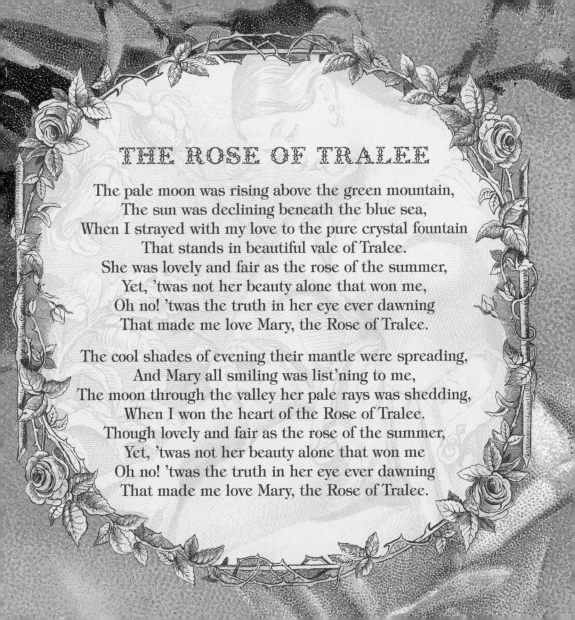

THE ROSE OF TRALEE

The pale moon was rising above the green mountain,
The sun was declining beneath the blue sea,
When I strayed with my love to the pure crystal fountain
That stands in beautiful vale of Tralee.
She was lovely and fair as the rose of the summer,
Yet, 'twas not her beauty alone that won me,
Oh no! 'twas the truth in her eye ever dawning
That made me love Mary, the Rose of Tralee.

The cool shades of evening their mantle were spreading,
And Mary all smiling was list'ning to me,
The moon through the valley her pale rays was shedding,
When I won the heart of the Rose of Tralee.
Though lovely and fair as the rose of the summer,
Yet, 'twas not her beauty alone that won me
Oh no! 'twas the truth in her eye ever dawning
That made me love Mary, the Rose of Tralee.

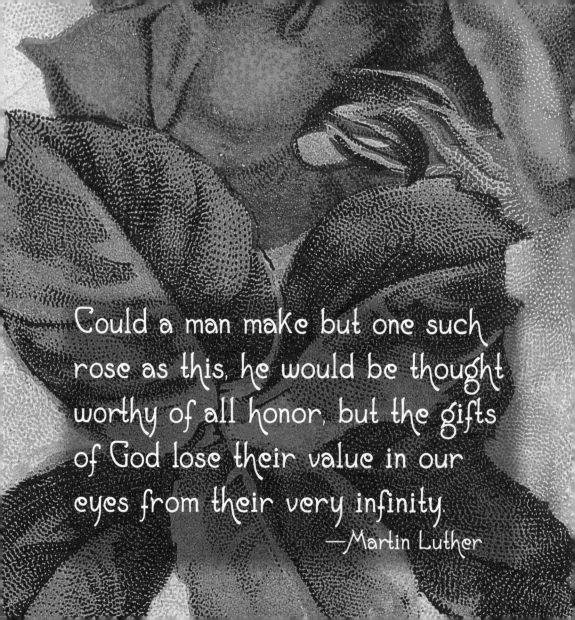

Could a man make but one such rose as this, he would be thought worthy of all honor, but the gifts of God lose their value in our eyes from their very infinity.

—Martin Luther

The War of the Roses

In the mid-fifteenth century, as the Hundred Years War between England and France was coming to a close, a new civil war in England was brewing between two powerful houses with claims to the English throne, the House of York and the House of Lancaster. This clash of nobles, which lasted from 1455 to 1485, became known as the War of the Roses, after the badges that represented each family. The white rose symbolized the House of York, while the red rose later came to represent the House of Lancaster.

In 1436, Richard, Duke of York, was next in line for the throne when he was sent by his cousin, King Henry VI of the house of Lancaster, to France to finance and maintain English interests in the Hundred Years War.

In 1445, the King replaced Richard in France with his close ally, Edmund, Duke of Somerset, who recommended exiling Richard by sending him to a new post in Ireland. Richard hated Edmund for having the

The War of the Roses

throne's support despite the fact that Edmund was losing ground in France. Meanwhile, the emotionally unstable Henry went insane causing him to suffer from paralysis in 1453. That same year, Queen Margaret gave birth to a son, Edward, guaranteeing the House of Lancaster's line of succession, but given Henry's illness, Richard was appointed Protector of England. The first thing he did was imprison Edmund for treason.

When Henry recovered two years later and took back control from Richard, he immediately released Edmund. But the battle lines of the War of the Roses were now drawn. Henry, his wife, Margaret, Edmund the Duke of Somerset, and the Earls of Northumberland became known as the Lancastrians after the House of Lancaster from which Henry descended; Richard and the Earls of Salisbury and Warwick were known as the Yorkists.

The first skirmish occurred that year at St. Albans, and Edmund was killed. Henry once again descended into mental illness and Margaret was left in charge of

The War of the Roses

the Lancastrians. Richard became Protector again for another year until 1456, when Henry declared himself fit to rule once again. Thus followed four years of relative peace, until 1460, when the houses battled again and Henry was captured.

Under pressure from the Yorkists, Parliament then passed an accord declaring Henry would remain king, but that after his death the throne would pass to Richard and his heirs. Queen Margaret, enraged that her son would be disinherited, raised an army to rescue Henry, in the second battle of St. Albans She defeated the Yorkists at Wakefield, where the Duke of York was killed. But she was ultimately defeated by the Yorkists at Mortimer's Cross.

Richard's son, Edward Plantagenet, assumed the throne in 1461 as Edward IV. Henry VI was briefly restored to the throne in 1470 with help from Louis XI of France, but Edward Plantagenet recaptured London and Henry a year later, and ruled for twelve years until his son, Edward V, succeeded him in 1483.

The War of the Roses

The next battle between the houses of York and Lancaster came when Edward's uncle, the Duke of Gloucester, usurped the throne and became King Richard III. Henry Tudor, Earl of Richmond—and Henry VI's illegitimate nephew—was the Lancastrian claimant at the time, and opposed Richard's rule. He defeated and killed Richard in 1485, and assumed the throne as Henry VII.

The houses of Lancaster and York were finally united under Tudor rule when King Henry VII married Edward IV's daughter, Elizabeth— effectively ending the War of the Roses. A red-and-white-striped rose, a symbol of the union between the two houses, represented the House of Tudor.

The Rose Family

The rose is a rose
And was always a rose,
But the theory now goes
That the apple's a rose,
And the pear is, and so's
The plum, I suppose.
The dear only knows
what will next prove a rose.
You, of course, are a rose—
But were always a rose.

—ROBERT FROST

Rose Ice Cream

1 TEASPOON SAFFRON
2 TABLESPOONS ROSE WATER (SEE P. 68 FOR RECIPE)
2 LARGE EGGS
$^3/_4$ CUP SUGAR
2 CUPS HEAVY CREAM, CHILLED
1 CUP SWEETENED CONDENSED MILK, CHILLED
$^3/_4$ CUP CHOPPED PISTACHIOS
$^1/_2$ CUP ORGANIC FRESH OR CANDIED ROSE PETALS, CHOPPED

1. In a small bowl, combine saffron and rose water and allow to sit overnight or, at minimum, 1 hour.
2. Before you continue with this recipe, make sure all ingredients are as cold as possible for best results.
3. In a large cold mixing bowl, beat the eggs until light and fluffy, about 2 minutes.

4. Slowly add sugar and continue beating until smooth, 1–2 minutes longer.
5. Add cream and condensed milk and beat until combined.
6. Strain saffron and add rose water to cream mixture.
7. Transfer mixture to an ice cream maker and freeze according to manufacturer's instructions.
8. Once the ice cream has stiffened and it is has only 45–90 seconds left, add chopped pistachios and rose petals and continue freezing until ice cream is ready.

Yields: 1 quart

Tess of the d'Urbervilles

by Thomas Hardy

Tess wished to abridge her visit as much as possible; but the young man was pressing, and she consented to accompany him. He conducted her around the lawns, and flowerbeds, and conservatories . . . and then the two passed round to the rosetrees, whence he gathered blossoms and gave her to put in her bosom. She obeyed like one in a dream, and when she could affix no more he himself tucked a bud or two into her hat, and heaped her basket with others in the prodigality of his bounty. . . .

Tess went down the hill to Trantridge Cross, and inattentively waited to take her seat in the van returning from Chaseborough to Shaston. She did not know what the other occupants said to her as she entered, though she answered them; and when they had started anew she rode along with an inward and not an outward eye.

One among her fellow-travelers addressed her more pointedly than any had spoken before: "Why, you be quite a posy! And such roses in early June!

Then she became aware of the spectacle she presented to their surprised vision: roses at her breast; roses in her hat, roses and strawberries in her basket to the brim. She blushed, and said confusedly that the flowers had been given to her. When the passengers were not looking she stealthily removed the more prominent blooms from her hat and placed them in the basket, where she covered them with her handkerchief. Then she fell to reflecting again, and in looking downwards, a thorn of the rose remaining in her breast accidentally pricked her chin. Like all the cottagers in Blackmoor Vale, Tess was steeped in fancies and prefigurative superstitions; she thought this an ill omen—the first she had noticed that day. 🌿

Oh! No man knows
Through what wild centuries
Roves back the rose.
—Walter de la Mare

Hesperides

Roses at first were white,
Till they could not agree
Whether my Sappho's breast
Or they more white should be. . . .
But being vanquished quite,
A blush their cheeks bespread;
Since which, believe the rest,
The roses first came red.

—ROBERT HERRICK

Roses

by Eleanor Perényi

Dreadful confession for a gardener to make, my favorite rose bush is an artificial one. Made of pure gold, crumpled and pleated and adorned with a single cabochon sapphire, this masterpiece of fifteenth-century jewelwork was the gift of Aeneas Pius Piccolomini, that most sympathetic of Renaissance popes and memoirists, to his native Siena. It is just under life size, about two feet high, and realistic enough to identify as an alba, yet it is an altogether poetic conception no real rose tree could match. Or so I feel after some thirty years of looking after countless specimens of the real thing. There are times when I long for a Midas touch to transform them into artifacts and relieve me of their care.

Four rectangular rose beds were in place when we bought the property, stocked with relics of many years' neglect. I haven't much recollection of them. I knew nothing about roses in those days, but I do remember that they gave us little trouble, and so I guess that most of them were what we call old-fashioned, a vague term that generally refers to roses bred before 1900. The lone survivor, whose age I can't guess, is a cabbage or Provence type, and it is still going strong. The others may have been of the same vintage. In any case, they wintered without protection, and were free alike from aphids and black spot. We rather despised them.

Roses

They didn't look half as glamorous as those we saw in the catalogues—modern hybrids elegant in form and exciting in color—and most of them bloomed intermittently, if at all, after the June outburst. So we got rid of what may have been an interesting collection, and thereby embarked on the slavery of watering, mulching, pruning, spraying for pests and diseases, that is the price of growing the modern hybrids. We hadn't anticipated that. My father managed the roses, and it was for him to learn the hard way how to cope with Japanese beetle traps, canvas hoses supposed to soak the soil without dampening the leaves, and defective sprayers. To him, it was worth it. He loved roses (many men do, for some reason), and cosseted his favorites: red-and-gold Condesa de Sastago, white Frau Druschki, above all that favorite of retired warriors, Peace—introduced in 1945.

Peace has a romantic story. It was bred by the distinguished French house of Meilland. In 1939, when Francis Meilland discovered in his nursery a ravishing rose growing from a single seed he had planted, he knew he had something extraordinary. The beginning of the war kept him from finding out exactly what. All he could do was to ship unnamed and largely untested cuttings in

199

all directions, hoping that one or another of them would arrive safely and survive. Those consigned to the American grower Robert Pyle, in Pennsylvania, were aboard the last plane to leave France in November 1940, a step ahead of the Nazi armies. The Meillands waited for four years to learn its fate, until August 1944, when a letter arrived from Pyle. 'Whilst dictating this letter,' he wrote, 'my eyes are fixed in fascinated admiration on a glorious rose, its pale gold, cream and ivory petals blended to a lightly ruffled edge of delicate carmine. There it is before me, full of promise, and I am convinced it will be the greatest rose of the century.'

He was right. Peace was skillfully promoted. On the day Berlin fell, it was given its name at a ceremony in California, attended by rose-lovers from all over the country, at which doves were set free. When the delegates to the San Francisco Conference arrived in their hotel rooms, each found a vase containing a single specimen, and a message from the American Rose Society conveying wishes for peace and good will. But in spite of the rather crass exploitation of the name (in Germany it was called Gloria Dei, in Italy Gioia, in France simply Mme. A. Meilland), Peace deserved its acclaim as the archetypal modern rose. The pity is that it should also have the archetypal modern faults. Beautiful though it is, it has no scent; and while it is fairly hardy, it is susceptible to every rose plague in the book. It was bred for looks alone and that, by and large, has been the aim of all modern breeders.

Roses

Peace is a hybrid tea, a class introduced about a century ago, and the most widely grown rose today. The others are the floribundas, developed in the 1920's, and the grandifloras, which date from 1954. Neither is an improvement in my opinion. The floribundas (crosses of the hybrid tea and the polyantha) bloom in multiple clusters and are slightly hardier than the hybrid tea. They are nice for picking because one cut procures a whole bouquet; but they, too, have been steadily deprived of scent, and they lack the elegance of the hybrid tea. The grandifloras I haven't a good word to say for. To me, they personify every wrong tendency in rose breeding, beginning with the pointless pursuit of novelty for its own sake. They are a recross of floribundas with hybrid teas, which causes them to produce flowers that bloom in clusters like the floribunda's, only slightly larger. There are no singles (a loss), and they have a narrower color range than either parent. Few have any perfume worth speaking of; and of all the unwelcome attributes in an age of smaller gardens, the bushes can be enormous.

At the other end of the scale from these monsters are the miniatures. These have their uses as pot plants (which is what they really are), but to promote them for beds and borders, as I constantly see done, is scandalous. The tallest is less than a foot high; yet because they are roses like any others, they, too, must be deadheaded, sprayed and fertilized—presumably from a prone position. To pretend that they are suitable for gardens in the last quarter of the twentieth century, when the luckiest of

Roses

us is dependent on the part-time services of a slouching adolescent or a senior citizen dying on his feet, when many gardeners are senior citizens themselves, is a pathetic example of how a business can lose touch with its logical clientele. Why not admit that they aren't for gardens, where few people plant them anyway? They are most often sold as single specimens, 'conversation pieces,' or as florist's offerings for Mother's Day. (One baby polyantha is called Mother's Day. Another is Happy, after one of the Seven Dwarfs—need one say more?)

The search for new colors isn't of the same order of folly. It is, or was, a pursuit that added many beautiful shades to the repertory, particularly among the golds and yellows. The first true yellow garden rose was Soleil d'Or, a hybrid tea introduced about 1910 by the French breeder Pernet-Ducher. Rose lovers owe so much to the French, whose preëminence goes back to the late Middle Ages, and who have been responsible for every major development up to and including the hybrid tea, that I often want to remind them of that old Gallic adage, *Le mieux est l'ennemi du bien*, which roughly translates as, Let well enough alone. I am thinking just now of Ambassador, a Meilland grandiflora proudly introduced by Wayside in the 1980 catalogue. Ambassador is a glistening apricot and could be considered gorgeous if experience

hadn't made me wary of its 'fashionable orangey color.' This range, a clamoring chorus of Sunkist oranges and corals, has increased by leaps and bounds since the 1960's. Katharine S. White (*Onward and Upward in the Garden*) was, I think, the first to object to them, pointing out that they look hideous planted with other, traditionally colored roses, and alongside a lot of other flowers as well. They need a bed apart, near marigolds or tiger lilies, and even then their autumnal colors are a jarring note in a summer garden. But worse is to come. We are promised a brown (or tan) rose someday. That sounds to me like something Chanel would have wanted to go with her Coromandel screens, not a garden flower. The rose world, like Detroit, seems to have put its faith in perpetually new 'styling' to attract a fickle public, and I predict that the results will be the same.

To a great extent, they already are. Statistics show that rose-growing is in decline in this country and has been for a long while. Wayside's catalogue for 1960 had thirty pages devoted to roses; in 1981, there were ten. Jackson & Perkins, once synonymous with roses, has drastically reduced its catalogue and has diversified into other plants. Still other companies have gone out of business. Books talk of some 5,000 varieties being available. I would like to know where. The average gardener who orders from catalogues, or shops at garden centers and nurseries, has access to a couple of dozen at most, and I sense that the supply more than meets the demand. People have lost interest in roses. Partly this is

Roses

due to the difficulties of growing them, which breeders have done little to alleviate. They don't seem to realize that most gardeners haven't time to embark on elaborate programs of spraying and fertilizing, and that environmentally sensitive gardeners refuse to spray, whether they have time or not. All that is out of date. And so, in a curious way, are the roses themselves with their neon colors and disappointing fragrance.

Again, the resemblance to the American car is striking. Not for nothing was a well-known modern rose called Chrysler Imperial. It was christened in 1952, the heyday of the overgrown gas guzzler with fins. Perhaps a plant ought not to be made to bear the burden of a breeder's bad taste in nomenclature. On the other hand, there is more than a casual relationship between the two. A flower whose grower thinks of it in terms of advertising and brand names ceases to be a flower and becomes a product to be marketed like any other. So it proved. Until recently, dozens of new models were introduced every year, heavily promoted and allowed to lapse from sight. It often happened that a rose one liked couldn't be replaced after a year or two. Rejection by the public may have been one factor, but there were disturbing analogies with a policy of planned obsolescence. Modern hybrid roses, like modern appliances, seem made not to last. Either they succumb to cold—and I find it ridiculous that living as I do on a coastal area of the moderate Zone 6, I should have to smother bushes in salt hay and wrap the standards like mummies or bury them alive—or they suffer from premature senility.

Roses

There are signs that the rose industry may be seeing the error of its ways. Although there is still talk of finding a better spray for black spot, a rose with inbred resistance to the disease is also being worked on. Bowing to the howls of rose lovers, some breeders are also trying to recapture lost perfume. For two decades, 'moderate' or 'slight' fragrance have been code words for 'little' or 'none.' 'Strong' is now beginning to appear in catalogues. Usually, it is an exaggeration, but it does signify a change of heart.

It may be too late to bring the disaffected back into the fold. Many gardeners who still love roses have been turning back to the species, and to those old and now rare types bred before 1900 which some call 'heritage roses.' I haven't the statistics but I would venture that they are the only roses whose cultivation is increasing. Certainly the catalogues that carry them are as fat as ever. The best known, *Roses of Yesterday and Today*, put out by the late Will Tillotson's firm in California, had more than two hundred entries in 1980, the majority of them roses of yesterday.

. . . . It seems to me that no clear choice is possible. Growing the European roses bred before 1800 is inevitably tempting to romantics, who get a thrill from their very names: White Rose of York, Rosa Mundi (believed to have been named for Rosamund, mistress of Henry

Roses

II), Rose of Castile. Having gone through this phase, I know the satisfactions. I also know that rose beds filled with very large bushes that won't bloom more than once a summer quickly become a bore. A shrub or two of these is sufficient, and not in beds. The same goes for the species. My Blanc Double de Coubert, a double rugosa originally planted in a bed, now occupies a space some four-by-eight feet near the garden shed, and is still sending up canes. It smells like the distillation of a million apple blossoms and can be detected a good fifty feet away. But it blooms in June, and hardly at all thereafter.

The nineteenth-century hybrids, which must be carefully selected according to one's climate zone, are much more rewarding and I always try to have a few in the beds. They are to the garden what fine antique furniture is to the house. They give it distinction. But the truth is I can't bring myself to turn my back entirely on modern roses. Standard bushes, which I persist in growing, are always grafts either of hybrid teas or the polyantha called the Fairy (which I reject). Then every so often a catalogue will turn up a rose that isn't to be resisted at any price. Last year, it was a hybrid tea called Paradise, a deep lavender suffused with ruby, and something close to an authentic tea scent. I don't suppose it will last. I don't, at this writing, even know if it is alive or dead under the snow of this exceptionally cold winter. But I had to have it. When it comes to roses, some of us are incurable.

Fighting Japanese Beetles

Japanese Beetles have long been recognized as the rose's number one nemesis. Devoted rose growers everywhere have at one time or another cursed the gods and stamped their feet in outrage upon sighting these nasty little creatures. Although they are a notoriously stubborn insect, here a few suggestions to help keep your garden beetle-free.

🦐

Consult your local nursery for the best way to treat your lawn for beetle grubs. This preventative measure will cut down the number of beetles in the future.

🦐

Plant flowers rich in pollen and nectar, such as daisies and asters. These blooms will attract wasps and flies that are natural predators of the Japanese Beetle.

🦐

Spray infested rose bushes with *neem*, a low-toxic biodegradable insecticide.

🦐

If all else fails, plant roses that bloom only once a year before the July beetle season.

un(bee)mo

vi
n(in)g
are(th
e)you(o
nly)

asl(rose)eep

—E.E. CUMMINGS

The Colors of The Rose

A quick trip to your local florist gives only an inkling about the variety of colors of roses available. Although red, pink, yellow, and white tea roses might be the standard when considering a bouquet, the combinations of colors found in a rose garden can be nearly infinite. Here is a sampling of the diverse and complex colors roses have been known to have:

Pure white ❀ Snow white ❀ Creamy white blushed with yellow ❀ Bright white touched with faintest peach ❀ Creamy white flushed with delicate pink, revealing brilliant golden centers ❀ Ivory with hints of amber ❀ Parchment with buff tints ❀ Cream with shades of copper ❀ Deep ivory blushed with brownish pink ❀ Clear pink ❀ Light pink with a white petal edge ❀

The Colors of The Rose

Cherry pink ❧ Deep crimson red ❧ Bright vermilion-orange ❧ rich, ruby red ❧ Deep beetroot purple ❧ Lavender fading to gray ❧ Lilac purple flushed with blue-pink, clear bright yellow ❧ Pale butter yellow ❧ Light yellow with palest green ❧ Warm apricot touched with orange ❧ Canary yellow with red ❧ Golden yellow infused with pink ❧ Buff yellow aging to pink and then slate purple ❧ Rich mauve aging to deep burgundy ❧ Magenta with violet veins, fading to grayish purple ❧ Rich blood red with shades of brown ❧ Orange-yellow with reddish-pink veins ❧ Hot pink ❧ Milky white with cerise edges ❧ Palest tan blushing pink and red ❧ Baby pink with blue undertones

THE YELLOW ROSE OF TEXAS

There's a yellow rose in Texas that I am going there to see,
No other soldier knows her, No soldier only me;
She cried so when I left her, it was like to broke my heart,
And if I ever find her we never more will part.

Chorus
She's the sweetest little flower this soldier ever knew,
Her eyes are bright as diamonds, they sparkle like the dew,
You may talk about your Dearest May, and sing of Rosa Lee,
But the yellow rose of Texas beats the belles of Tennessee.

Where the Rio Grande is flowing, and the starry skies are bright,
She walks along the river in the quiet summer night;
She thinks if I remember when we parted long ago,
I promised to come back again, and not to leave her so.

Oh, now I'm going to find her, for my heart is full of woe,
And we'll sing the song together, that we sung so long ago;
We'll play the banjo gaily, and we'll sing the songs of yore,
And the Yellow Rose of Texas,
shall be mine forevermore.

Love in the Time of Cholera

by Gabriel García Marquez

O ne morning, as he was cutting roses in his garden, Florentino Ariza could not resist the temptation of taking one to [Fermina Daza] on his next visit. It was a difficult problem in the language of flowers because she was a recent widow. A red rose, symbol of flaming passion, might offend her mourning. Yellow roses, which in another language were the flowers of good fortune, were an expression of jealousy in the common vocabulary. He had heard of the black roses of Turkey, which was perhaps the most appropriate, but he had not been able to obtain any for acclimatization in his patio. After much thought he risked a white rose, which he like less than the others because it was insipid and mute: it did not say anything. At the last minute, in case Fermina Daza was suspicious enough to attribute some meaning to it, he removed the thorns.

It was well received as a gift with no hidden intentions, and the Tuesday ritual was enriched, so that when he would arrive with the white rose, the vase with water was ready in the center of the tea table. One Tuesday, as he placed the rose in the vase, he said in an apparently casual manner:

"In our day it was camellias, not roses."

"That is true," she said, "but the intention was different, and you know it."

Rose Preserves

3 CUPS ORGANIC ROSE PETALS
$1/2$ CUP WATER
JUICE OF 1 LEMON
2 CUPS GRANULATED SUGAR
1 PACKAGE SURE-JELL PECTIN (OR SIMILAR PRODUCT)

1. Begin by sterilizing four 8-ounce jars and lids in a large pot of boiling water for 5–10 minutes. Handle with care.
2. Combine 2 cups rose petals, water, and lemon juice in a blender or food processor and blend until smooth. Add sugar through feed hole until combined.
3. Pour mixture into a heavy-bottomed saucepan and bring to a boil over medium-high heat, stirring occasionally.
4. As bubbles begin to form, add pectin and remaining rose petals. Stir constantly.
5. Boil for 1 minute and remove from heat. Pour into jars and seal.
7. Invert jars for the first 20 minutes and then place, right side up, in your refrigerator to cool completely.

If stored properly, this jam will keep for 1–2 months.

The Rose Talks Back

I hate the man who builds his name
On ruins of another's fame.
Thus prudes, by characters o'erthrown,
Imagine that they raise their own.
Thus scribblers, covetous of praise,
Think slander can transplant the bays.
Beauties and bards have equal pride,
With both all rivers are decried . . .

As in the cool of early day
A poet sought the sweets of May,
The garden's fragrant breath ascends,
And ev'ry stalk with odor bends.
A rose he plucked, he gazed, admired,

Thus singing as the Muse inspired:
"Go, rose, my Chloe's bosom grace;
How happy should I prove;
Might I supply that envied place
With never-fading love!
There, Phoenix-like, beneath her eye,
Involved in fragrance, burn and die!

"Know, hapless flower, that thou shalt find
More fragrant roses there;
I see thy with'ring head reclined
With envy and despair!
One common fate we both must prove;
You die with envy, I with love."

"Spare your comparisons," replied
An angry Rose who grew beside.
"Of all mankind, you should not flout us;
What can a poet do without us?
In ev'ry love song roses bloom,
We lend you color and perfume.
Does it to Chloe's charms conduce
To found her praise on our abuse?
Must we, to flatter her, be made
To wither, envy, pine and fade?"

—JOHN GAY

Carefree Roses

Even if you don't have a lot of time to spend on your roses, you still can enjoy them. There are many relatively carefree varieties from which to choose. In general, old or ancient breeds are extremely disease resistant and relatively easy to grow. The Alba rose, known as the healthiest of all the ancient roses, will even tolerate partial shade. The main drawback is that ancient roses generally bloom only once a year, in the spring, and then set rose hips in the fall. A gardener looking to have blooms throughout the growing season might want to invest in some of the modern hybrids that have been bred to bloom repeatedly and require a minimum of care.

Red

Dortmund: This rugged climber makes a beautiful crimson cover for an archway or pergola. Tolerant of shade and a repeat bloomer, this rose is another great disease resistant choice if you are looking for lovely red blooms for your garden.

Herbstfeuer: This stunning red hybrid is also called 'Autumn Fire' for the spectacular hips and golden foliage it produces in

Carefree Roses

the fall. With full and very fragrant blooms, *Herbstfeuer* will rebloom throughout the summer, and its hardy leaves rarely fall prey to black spot, an unusual benefit for a rose of this color.

PINK

The Fairy: This polyantha with clusters of delicate, pink double blooms is practically indestructible, hardy to zone 4. A low, spreading shrub that will grow two to three feet tall with a three- to four-foot spread, the Fairy blooms continuously throughout the season.

Carefree Beauty: A shrub rose with semi-double, pale pink flowers, this repeat-blooming rose is vigorous and spreading, reaching heights of five to six feet. It is hardy to zones 4 or 5 and its olive-green foliage is highly disease resistant.

Queen Elizabeth: This pink, blissfully scented grandiflora is suited to first-timers. The repeat-blooming flowers make an excellent cutting rose and the leathery leaves resist disease. It is hardy to zone 6 and grows to five to seven feet in height and two to three feet in width.

Great Maiden's Blush: This exquisitely fragrant shell pink Alba rose grows vigorously even in partial shade and gravelly soils. Its lovely blue-gray leaves make it a beautiful shrub even when not in bloom,

Carefree Roses

and its once yearly flowering produces roses with 40 petals per blossom. This tough beauty thrives in zones 3 through 10 and has excellent disease resistance.

New Dawn: A beautiful climbing rose with pale pink flowers that rebloom throughout the summer, New Dawn grows vigorously and produces shining, deep green leaves. Occasionally susceptible to mildew, this winter-hardy flower is perfect for trellises and arbors.

Ballerina: A hybrid musk that bears clouds of delicate pink flowers all summer long, Ballerina tolerates Southern heat well and is highly resistant to disease. Simply feed and water regularly to keep her blooming prodigiously.

Stanwell Perpetual: A repeat flowering species cross, this rose begins bearing doubled blush pink flowers early in the season. Stanwell Perpetual is not susceptible to black spot or mildew, and is hardy in zones 4 though 10.

Jens Munk: This thorny beauty is extremely hardy, thriving even in windy, salty, and drought-prone places. Flowering continuously with large, heavily perfumed bright lavender pink blossoms, Jens Munk is nearly immune to disease.

Carefree Roses

White

Alba Semi-Plena (The White Rose of York): Cultivated for centuries for its *attar*, or fragrant essential oil, these semi-double blossoms have beautiful, disease-resistant gray-green foliage with many prickles. The creamy semi-double flowers bloom once a season and the plant is hardy to zones 3 to 4.

Blanc Double de Coubert: One of the few truly white roses, this hybrid rugosa bears tissue-thin double blossoms throughout the season. In the fall, its wrinkly green leaves turn a lovely gold and then purple, producing rosy scarlet hips. This rugosa needs no pruning and will reach a height of five feet.

Sea Foam: This shrub rose makes a wonderful ground cover and prefers full sun. Its repeating double blooms are white with a hint of pink, and the leathery green foliage is highly resistance to disease.

Multicolored

Rosa Mundi: Also called *Rosa gallica versicolor*, this rose has been cultivated since the 1500s and bears large fragrant blossoms once per

Carefree Roses

season, in early spring. The flowers are striped with white, pink, and red, and the plant makes a wonderful low hedge with few thorns.

Ferdinand Pichard: This hybrid perpetual shrub rose produces full pink and red striped blossoms, with three to five flowers per stem. Though somewhat susceptible to black spot, the large blooms are extraordinarily fragrant and hardy from zones 5 through 10. If you deadhead regularly, this rose will rebloom all summer.

COPPER

Hawaiian Sunset: This coppery hybrid tea makes the perfect choice for a cutting garden or rose bed. Hawaiian Sunset grows dense, dark green foliage and is not prone to pests or mildew. It blooms in spring and late summer.

YELLOW

Danaë: Known as the healthiest yellow repeat-blooming rose, this lightly scented hybrid musk produces delicate semi-double blossoms continuously through the summer. Great for mixed border plantings, *Danaë*'s glossy green foliage is only slightly susceptible to black spot.

What would the rose with all
her pride be worth,
Were there no sun to call
her brightness forth?

—Thomas Moore

Seasoned and Safe Roses

by Richardson Wright

If I were genuine, sincere and rabid Rosarian (and could afford to satisfy my whims) I would order Rose nurserymen to send me every new hybrid that comes their way. And what an utter fool I'd be! There is no easier method of becoming disillusioned about Roses and no simpler way of parting with your hard-earned shekels. Rose enthusiasm has waxed to that point where the subtlest variation will throw catalogue writers into ecstasies and rob their pens of adjectives. Having been many times burned by these, I am thrice shy. I have reached the same determination about Roses that I have about investments: I want them seasoned and safe. I'm not interested in a Rose unless it has been on the market five years. In fact, the very next Rose order that leaves this house has a "stop" on it at 1900 and some of the items go back to the 1500's. Let others toy with the subtleties, idiosyncrasies and delicacies of the latest hybrid teas, we shall devote our Rose space to Damask and Gallica, Provence and Moss Roses. And, incidentally, we will have fragrance. 🌿

The Sensitive Plant

And the rose like a nymph to
the bath addressed,
Which unveiled the depth
of her glowing breast,
Till, fold after fold, to the
fainting air
The soul of her beauty and
love lay bare;

—PERCY BYSSHE SHELLEY

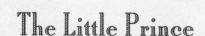

The Little Prince

by Antoine de Saint-Exupéry

The little prince went to look at the roses again.

"You're not at all like my rose. You're nothing at all yet," he told them. "No one has tamed you and you haven't tamed anyone. You're the way my fox was. He was just a fox like a hundred thousand others. But I've made him my friend, and now he's the only fox in all the world."

And the roses were humbled.

"You're lovely, but you're empty," he went on. "One couldn't die for you. Of course, an ordinary passerby would think my rose looked just like you. But my rose, all on her own, is more important than all of you together, since she's the one I've watered. Since she's the one I put under glass. Since she's the one I sheltered behind a screen. Since she's the one for whom I killed the caterpillars (except the two or three for butterflies). Since she's the one I listened to when she complained, or when she boasted, or even sometimes when she said nothing at all. Since she's *my* rose."

And he went back to the fox.

"Good-bye," he said.

"Good-bye," said the fox. "Here is my secret. It's quite simple: One sees clearly only with the heart. Anything essential is invisible to the eyes."

The Little Prince

~

"I'm thirsty for that water," said the little prince. "Let me drink some . . ."

And I understood what he'd been looking for!

I raised the bucket to his lips. He drank, eyes closed. It was as sweet as a feast. That water was more than merely a drink. It was born of our walk beneath the stars, of the song of the pulley, of the effort of my arms. It did the heart good, like a present. When I was a little boy, the Christmas-tree lights, the music of midnight mass, the tenderness of people's smiles made up, in the same way, the whole radiance of the Christmas present I received.

"People where you live," the little prince said, "grow five thousand roses in one garden . . . yet they don't find what they 're looking for . . ."

"They don't find it," I answered.

"And yet what they're looking for could be found in a single rose, or a little water . . ."

"Of course," I answered.

And the little prince added, "But eyes are blind. You have to look with the heart."

Little Known Rose Facts

Aphrodite's son Eros, the god of sexual desire, has been depicted wearing a crown of roses.

The rose is the National Floral Emblem of the United States, and is the state flower of Georgia, Iowa, New York, North Dakota, and the District of Columbia.

Sufi poetry from the 11th century describes roses as a symbol of life: the beauty of the rose represented life's perfection, and the thorns of the rose represented the difficulties in life one must overcome to achieve perfection.

Centerfolia, Damask, and Gallica roses are the most commonly grown commercial roses

Little Known Rose Facts

In his writings, Confucius states that the emperor of China owned over six hundred books about roses. Rose oil extracted from the blooms in the emperor's garden could only be used by nobles and dignitaries; a peasant found in possession of the oil would be put to death.

In Renaissance times, fresh roses were prized after the summer months. People stored sand-filled clay pots stuffed with rosebuds in cool streams to keep them fresh until they needed them.

People value rose oil for its anti-inflammatory effect as well as its ability to lift the spirit and reduce depression and stress.

Beloved for their beauty and grace, revered as sacred to the gods, and coveted for their scent and healing oils, roses have been cultivated by civilizations around the globe since ancient times. The rose that most people think of today, with a high center and multiple petals, is a relatively new arrival in the global garden. Developed in 1867, the hybrid tea rose "La France" marked the evolution from the "Old Roses"—garden roses with a single layer of five petals that bloomed once a year—to the modern hybrid roses with fuller blossoms blooming many times in a season.

Though geological evidence suggests that roses graced the earth prior to humans, our first representations of this mythic flower come from the 12th-century-b.c. Persians, who carved the five-petaled rose as a religious symbol. Later, in the 10th century B.C., the Greeks considered the heavenly scented

The History of the Rose

Damask rose growing on the island of Samos sacred to their goddess Aphrodite. The Romans were equally enamored of roses, creating hothouses so that they would have a constant supply, and even importing the plants from Egypt. Reportedly, Emperor Nero even covered an entire beach with rose petals during an extravagant celebration.

During the Middle Ages, roses were cultivated in church and monastery gardens,

harvested not only for the beauty of their fragrant blossoms, but also for the medicinal properties of their petals. Oils, pastes, and powders made from the "Apothecary's Rose" were used to cure everything from skin afflictions to eye disease, and the therapeutic properties of the rose are recognized to this day. Up to 18th century, there were fewer than 30 varieties of roses. This all changed when the Dutch became the first Europeans to breed and cultivate new varieties of roses from seed. Empress Josephine fueled the popularity of roses in France in the 1800s, creating the first all-rose garden at her palace, Malmaison, where several new breeds were developed.

Roses from the Orient became all the rage in the mid-nineteenth century because of their ability to bloom continuously, and these roses were crossbred with "Old Roses" to produce a new generation of hybrids. Though popular for their high centers and multiple petals, these new hybrids also introduced diseases not previously encountered in European varieties. Because these blossoms were in fashion for indoor bouquets, gardeners cared less about the hardiness of the plants themselves than the quality of the cut flowers.

Times change, however, and today's gardeners focus on producing healthy, hearty plants that produce the stunning blossoms that have inspired poets, priests, and the people of the world for centuries.

Rose, Round Whose Bed

Rose, round whose bed
Dawn's cloudlets close,
Earth's brightest-bred
Rose!

No song, love knows,
May praise the head
Your curtain shows.

Ere sleep has fled,
The whole child glows
One sweet live red
Rose.

—ALGERNON SWINBURNE

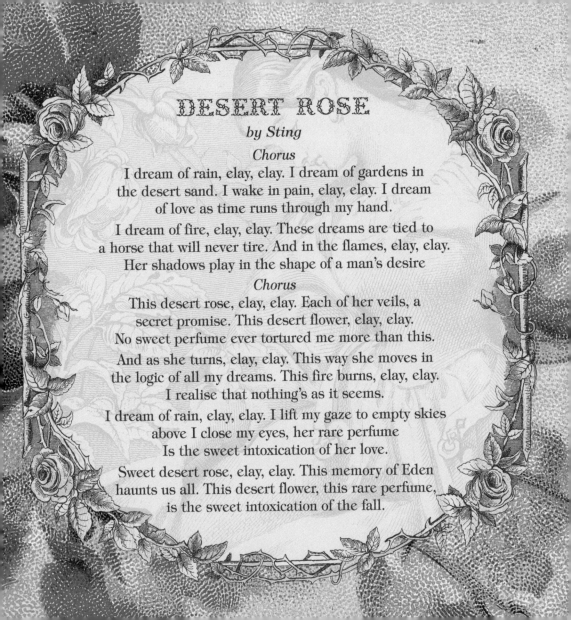

DESERT ROSE

by Sting

Chorus

I dream of rain, elay, elay. I dream of gardens in
the desert sand. I wake in pain, elay, elay. I dream
of love as time runs through my hand.

I dream of fire, elay, elay. These dreams are tied to
a horse that will never tire. And in the flames, elay, elay.
Her shadows play in the shape of a man's desire

Chorus

This desert rose, elay, elay. Each of her veils, a
secret promise. This desert flower, elay, elay.
No sweet perfume ever tortured me more than this.

And as she turns, elay, elay. This way she moves in
the logic of all my dreams. This fire burns, elay, elay.
I realise that nothing's as it seems.

I dream of rain, elay, elay. I lift my gaze to empty skies
above I close my eyes, her rare perfume
Is the sweet intoxication of her love.

Sweet desert rose, elay, elay. This memory of Eden
haunts us all. This desert flower, this rare perfume,
is the sweet intoxication of the fall.

Rose Essence and Rose Oil

Pure rose oil is also called "otto of roses" or "attar of roses" which is from the Farsi word, atar, meaning "perfume," and the Arabic itr, "to smell sweet." Rose oil is a favorite perfume, and has been a plant used in healing since the time of Hippocrates. It was prescribed for nausea, stomachache, infections, and as a hangover cure. Rub rose oil into the temples for a headache, or on hands and feet to relieve the pains of arthritis.

In 1639, Philbert Guibert, Esq., Physician Regent of Paris, France wrote, "To make Oyle of Roses take a pound of red rose petals, beat them in a marble morter with a wooden pestle, then put them in an earthen pot, and pour upon them four pound of oyle of olives, letting them infuse the space of a month in the sunne, or in the chimney corner, stirring of them sometimes. Then heat it, and press it and strain it, and put it into the same pot or other vessel to keep."

Rose Essence and Rose Oil

A more modern method for obtaining true rose oil is the process of distillation by solvent:

1. After several sunny days, check your garden for roses that are open, but not yet beginning to fade in color. Pick them after the morning dew has dried, but before the sun is high. Red roses are usually the most fragrant. Use only garden roses that have not been sprayed with any chemicals. Commercial roses will not yield much essence.
2. Place eight ounces unflavored vodka in a clean 16-ounce jar. Cover the vodka with $1/2$ cup rose petals that have been rinsed and dried.
3. Cover tightly and let stand for two weeks.
4. Strain through cheesecloth into another jar, pressing the petals firmly to remove all the oil.
5. Freeze this liquid for 24 hours. The rose oil will rise to the top and freeze, but the vodka will not.
6. Remove the frozen oil (about an ounce) and place it in a small container with a tightly fitting lid.

Rose Infused Oil

You can make this easily with two ingredients and a bit of patience.

1. Place 4 ounces of light virgin olive oil or grapeseed oil in a clean glass jar, and cover it with rose petals.
2. Allow the petals to marinate in the oil for 24 hours.
3. Strain the mixture through cheesecloth, squeezing all the oil from the petals.
4. Add more fresh rose petals to the oil and repeat the process. Do this several times until the oil has the desired fragrance strength.
5. Store oil in an airtight container.

We all know persons who are affected for better or for worse by certain odors . . . Over and over again I have experienced the quieting influence of Rose scent upon a disturbed state of mind, feeling the troubled condition smoothing out before I realized that Roses were in the room, or near at hand.

—Louise Beebe Wilder

Sonnet 54

O! how much more doth beauty
    beauteous seem
By that sweet ornament which
    truth doth give!
The rose looks fair, but fairer
    we it deem
For that sweet odor, which doth
    in it live.

—WILLIAM SHAKESPEARE

The Fragrance of the Rose

The scent of the rose has been treasured for years for its powers of seduction, healing, and promotion of well being. Roses have been valued by many cultures throughout time, showing up in the tombs of Egyptian pharaohs, the mythology of the Greeks, the ceremonies of the Romans, and the writings of the Persians. All of these civilizations prized roses for their attar, or oil, and its ability to imbue a heavenly aroma into everything it touches.

The ancient Romans, famous for their indulgences in all things luxurious, specifically obsessed over the rose. They stuffed their pillows and mattresses with rose petals and watched plays in amphitheaters shaded by awnings soaked in rose perfume. Emperor Nero, known for his extravagance, showered rose petals and rose water on dinner guests, so many, in fact, that one person reportedly smothered.

The Fragrance of the Rose

Ancient Egyptians, Greeks, and Indians mashed fresh rose petals in hot fat to create delightfully scented pomades used to perfume the body. In Egypt, these pomades were shaped into cones and placed on the head. The person's body heat would melt the mixture, causing the rose-scented oil to trickle down the face and neck.

Legend has it though, that the Persians were the first to discover and bottle rose oil. They developed a crude distillation process to gather the essential oil and since nearly 60,000 blooms are required to produce just one ounce of oil, it became one of the most expensive substances on earth. Roses and their fragrance were prevalent in Islamic culture, taking on more of spiritual significance as rosewater was used in the mortar of temples. During the Crusades, knights brought back the scented oils that suggested all the seductive pleasures of the east and they became instantly popular.

During the Middle Ages, roses hearkened back to the hedonistic pagan cultures of the past and fell out of favor. Monasteries continued to grow roses for their medicinal properties, but it wasn't until the 1700s that

The Fragrance of the Rose

perfumes and scents regained their popularity. Members of the French nobility doused themselves in rose perfumes, and Empress Josephine cultivated every know variety of the bloom at her palace.

Despite all of the modern technologies available today, rose oil is extracted in much the same way as it was in ancient times. In Bulgaria, a country that produces the majority of the world's rose attar, roses are harvested by hand in the early morning hours in late May and June. The residents of Kazanluk, a town in central Bulgaria in a place known as the Valley of the Roses, send sacks of roses to distilleries to harvest the oil. It still takes more than 1,400 flowers to produce a gram of attar, or "liquid gold" as it is known in Bulgaria. Morocco, another of the world's largest rose cultivators, produces rose absolute, a form of rose oil. Rose absolute is obtained through a chemical refinement process that creates a concentration of aromatic compounds and essential oil.

The luscious and seductive scent of the rose is as popular now as it ever was, and equally as precious.

The Fragrance of the Rose

Rose oil is often used in modern perfumes in combination with other flower essences, and is used widely in aromatherapy for its calming, comforting, and balancing effects. The next time you apply your favorite rose scent, imagine yourself in the company of the ancient kings and queens from around the world, and revel in the intoxicating aroma of this timeless and delicate flower.

Asian Rose Vinegar

1$^1/_2$ CUPS ORGANIC ROSE PETALS
3 TABLESPOONS ROSE-COLORED "SZECHUAN" PEPPERCORNS
4 CUPS WHITE VINEGAR

1. Sterilize a large, clean glass bottle or jar in boiling water for 5–10 minutes.
2. Remove from water and cool slightly.
3. Pack bottle with rose petals and peppercorns, and then fill with white vinegar.
4. Let stand, undisturbed for 3–5 days at room temperature.
5. Once vinegar has taken on the color and fragrance of the roses, strain petals and peppercorns out.
6. Sterilize bottle or jar again, using the same process as earlier and refill with Rose Vinegar.

If properly stored and handled, vinegar will keep for 2–3 months.

He who must
have beautiful
roses in his
garden must
have beautiful
roses in his heart.

—S. Reynolds Hole

The Carolina Rose

With no recourse
She shines, fresh from the shower,
Webbed in diamonds,
Lustrous in the morning dew.

Roots delirious in mineral mud,
Companion to the neighboring bud
And withered blossom leaving,
She is the daughter of the one
Who shapes the roseate puffs of cloud,
A silent shimmering vision of gold
Expanding in the blue mandala evening.

When you breathe her fragrance
The moonbeams sing
The chorus of Orion's symphony,
The spinning song of nebulae—
Unfolding petals, petals unfolding
The radiant face of beauty.

—DAVID LAWSON

'Mme Hardy' and 'Cuisse de Nymphe'

by Michael Pollan

Up to now, I've always avoided growing roses—real roses, that is; I've always had a tough climber or two. After all, who courts such captious and intimidating guests? But this spring for some reason the ripe catalogue shots of roses I always used to sail right past took hold in my imagination, and I decided to take the plunge. I think it must have been the two-page spread of "old-fashioned" roses in the Wayside catalogue that first seduced me. Here were a dozen ladies (and one debonair gent: 'Jacques Cartier') that looked nothing like roses were supposed to look. Instead of the trite, chaste, florist-ship bud, these large, shrubby plants bore luxuriant blooms that seemed to cascade down from the page: unruly masses of flower petals—hundreds of petals in some of them—just barely contained by form, which in most cases was that of a rosette or a teacup's half-globe. The whole effect was vaguely lascivious.

Dazzled, smitten, I ordered four old roses from Wayside. 'Mme Hardy,' of course; 'Jacques Cartier,' an 1868 introduction who looks quite suave in all his pictures; 'Königin von Dänemark' ("a jewel beyond price," and so presumably a bargain at $17.75); and 'Blanc Double de Coubert,' an

'Mme Hardy' and 'Cuisse de Nymphe'

1892 hybrid rugosa that Gertrude Jekyll considered "the whitest rose known." From another firm, I ordered a rose Wayside did not then carry, 'Maiden's blush,' a shell-pink alba about which the catalogue copy was unequivocal: "Nature has created nothing more exquisite in plant or bloom."

The afternoon my old roses arrived by UPS truck, they seemed little more than sticks to me. They were completely dormant, and, apart from a faint swelling at the buds, they looked dead. Hard to believe I had dropped a total of seventy-five bucks on these twigs. The plants looked like two octopi joined at the head, the roots coming out one side and the canes the other. The idea, according to the directions, was to set the head (really the bud union) on top of a Connecticut garden, Wayside recommends burying the bud union of a new rosebush at least two inches beneath the surface to protect it from winter stress. I checked the depth of the holes I had dug, carefully placed each rose, and then filled with soil, administering a final deep soak to ensure complete contact between the roots and the surrounding earth. After a few days of moisture, the roses would break their dormancy. The roots would send their delicate tentacles deep into the underlying mound of earth, and the alchemy by which the rose promised to translate this black mass of manure and decayed vegetable matter into blooms of legendary beauty would begin.

'Mme Hardy' and 'Cuisse de Nymphe'

After only a few days, the buds reddened and swelled, and by the end of two weeks, the canes had unfurled around themselves a deep-green cloak of leaves—paler, daintier, and in finish more matte than the high-gloss foliage of modern roses. I had read that most old roses flower on "old wood" (last season's growth), so I had no expectation of blooms that first season. But in late June, after a month of rapid growth, 'Mme Hardy' sent forth a generous spray of buds. By then I had read so much about old roses that I frankly doubted they could live up to their billing. But 'Mme Hardy' was beautiful. From a small, undistinguished bud emerged a tightly wound bundle of pure, porcelain-white petals innumerable yet not merely a mass: more ladylike than that, the fine tissue of 'Mme Hardy's' petals was subtly composed into the quartered form of a rosette, and the blooms made me think of the rose windows of Gothic cathedrals, which had not before looked to me anything like a rose.

It was hard to look at 'Mme Hardy' plain, hard not to think of her as an expression of another time—which of course, as much as being an expression of nature, she is. Though 'Mme Hardy' did not appear until 1832 (bred by the Empress Josephine's head gardener at Malmaison, and named for his wife), she embodies the classic form of old roses, and comes closer to the image the word "rose" has conjured in people's minds for most of Western history than do the roses in our florist shops today. To look closely at the bloom of an antique rose is, at least in some small way, an exercise of the historical imagination. You see it through

your own eyes, yet also through the eyes of another time. What an odd thing, though, for a rose is not a poem, or a painting, but a flower, part of nature, timeless. Yet man in some sense made 'Mme Hardy,' crossed and recrossed it until it reflected his ideal of beauty—and so today in my garden it reflects the sensibility of another time back at me, a part of nature, but also a part of us.

Admiring the beauty of 'Mme Hardy' I began to see why she should so excite rosarians of a snobbish bent—and to accept the slightly uncomfortable fact that, at least in the war of the roses, my own sympathies were not with the party of the people. For, compared with modern roses, 'Mme Hardy' is indeed an aristocrat, incomparably more subtle and, in form, so much more poised, than, say, 'Dolly Parton,' with her huge blossoms.

Once you have grown old roses, you can begin to understand why people might project metaphors of social class onto them. Each bush itself forms a kind of social hierarchy. Beneath 'Mme Hardy's' bud union is the rootstock of another, tougher variety—not a hybrid but a rude species rose, some hardy peasant stock that can withstand bad winters, but whose meager flowers interest no one. The prized hybrid is grafted onto the back of this anonymous rootstock, which performs all the hard labor for the rose, working the soil, getting its roots dirty so that the plant may bloom. Although the prickly bush that results is not itself distinguished either, it, too, is necessary to support the luxury of the bloom. But the extravagant, splendid blooms, like true aristocrats, never seem to

'Mme Hardy' and 'Cuisse de Nymphe'

acknowledge the plant that supports them. They comport themselves as though their beauty and station were God-given, transcendent. You cannot discern in the bloom of a rose the work of the plant, the sacrifice of its chafer-eaten leaves, the stink of the manure in which it is rooted. "Roots?" 'Mme Hardy' asks ingenuously. "What roots?"

But if 'Mme Hardy' calls attention to her pedigree, 'Maiden's Blush,' the alba I planted beside her in my garden, seems to press her sexuality on us. Her petals are more loosely arrayed than 'Mme Hardy's,' less done up—almost unbuttoned. Her petals are larger, too, and they flush with the palest flesh-pink toward the center, which itself is elusive, concealed in the multiplication of her labial folds. The blush of this maiden is clearly not all in her face . . . Could I be imagining things? Well, consider some of the other names by which this rose is known: 'La Virginale,' 'Incarnata,' 'La Séduisante,' and . . . 'Cuisse de Nymphe.' This last is what the rose is called in France, where, as Vita Sackville-West tells us, blooms that blush a particularly deep pink are given the "highly expressive name" of 'Cuisse de Nymphe Emue,' which she demurs from translating. But there it is: the thigh of an aroused nymph.

To look at a flower and think of sex—what exactly can this mean? Emerson wrote that "Nature always wears the colors of the spirit," by which he meant that we don't see nature plain only through a

screen of human tropes. So, in our eyes, spring becomes youth, trees become truths, and even the humble ant becomes a big-hearted soldier. And certainly, when we look at roses and see aristocratic ladies or even Girl Scouts, or—on a higher level—symbols of love and purity, we are projecting human categories onto those roses, saddling them with the infinite burden of our metaphors.

In my garden this summer, 'Maiden's Blush' has flowered hugely, and some of her blossoms are flushed so deeply pink as to deserve the French appellation, 'Cuisse de Nymphe Emue.' Am I thinking metaphorically? Well, yes and no. This flower, like all flowers, is, after all a sexual organ. The unlettered bumblebee seems to find this bloom just as attractive as I do: he seems just as bowled over by its perfume. Yet I can't believe I gaze at the blossom in quite the same way he does. Its allure, for me, has to do with its resemblance to women—put frankly, to "the thighs of an aroused nymph," about which I must assume the bumblebee feels nothing. For this is a resemblance my species has bred this rose to have. So are my ideas imaginary? Merely a representation of my own psychology and desire? But what about the bee? That's no representation he is busy pollinating. Are we finally speaking of nature or culture when we speak of a rose (nature) that has been bred by men (culture) so that its blossoms (nature) make men imagine (culture) the sex of women (nature)?

It may be this sort of confusion that we need more of. Among plants, none supply it quite as well as the rose. 🌿

The Rose

A rose, as fair as ever saw the north,
Grew in a little garden all alone;
A sweeter flower did nature ne'er put forth,
Nor fairer garden yet was never known.
The maidens danced about it morn and noon,
And learnèd bards of it their ditties made;
The nimble fairies by the pale-faced moon
Watered the root and kissed her pretty shade.
But well-a-day!—the gardener careless grew;
The maids and fairies both were kept away,
And in a drought the caterpillars threw
Themselves upon the bud and every spray.
God shield the stock! If heaven send no supplies,
The fairest blossom of the garden dies.

—WILLIAM BROWNE

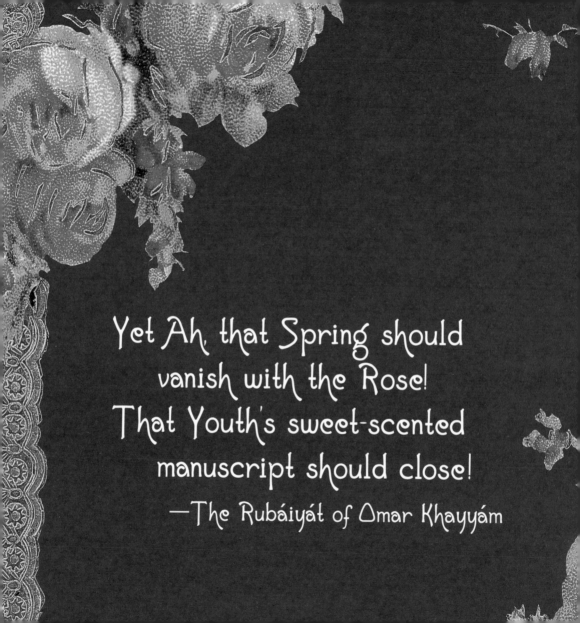

Yet Ah, that Spring should
vanish with the Rose!
That Youth's sweet-scented
manuscript should close!
—The Rubáiyát of Omar Khayyám

Rose Potpourri

Potpourri is the ancient art of mixing fragrant flowers and herbs with aromatic spices and oils. There are endless combinations to delight your sense of smell. You could use the roses from your wedding bouquet, from an anniversary, or a Valentine's Day gift. You can use the potpourri in a bowl on a table or shelf to perfume a room, sew some into a pillow, or fill a small cloth bag to hang in your closet. Place a handful in a handkerchief tied with a pretty ribbon to add fragrance to your dresser drawers.

A fixative like powdered orris root (from the iris plant), gum benzoin, callamus root, dry lavender, or oak moss must be added to dried flower petals to preserve their perfume. These can be found in herb shops, craft stores, and some drug stores.

Fragrant Rose Potpourri

3 dozen fresh roses
1 Tablespoon fixative
1 cup dried lime leaves
Several cinnamon sticks
1 Tablespoon whole cloves
10 whole nutmeg cloves
1/4 cup dried citrus peel
3 or 4 vanilla beans
Rose oil
Sandalwood oil

1. Collect roses when they are fully open, but have not yet turned brown. Dry the petals on a screen or a tray lined with brown paper in a warm, dry place until they turn crisp.
2. In a large bowl mix 1 quart dried petals with 1 tablespoon of fixative.
3. Add lime leaves and spices. Sprinkle with a few drops of the essential oils.
4. Place in a covered container for 10 days, shaking the contents daily.

Antique vs. Modern Roses

Rose lovers debate endlessly over which is better—Old Garden Roses or the modern Hybrid Tea Roses. The term "Old Garden Roses" refers to all roses grown before the first tea rose hybrid was introduced in 1867. "Hybrid Tea Roses" includes all the rose varieties bred since 1867. Those who prefer the old varieties of rose bushes say their blooms look more natural and beautiful, give more flowers, are more fragrant, and are more hardy and less prone to disease. Lovers of the Hybrid Teas state that the Hybrid Teas are more beautiful, produce larger flowers, provide a greater abundance of colors, and have a much longer blooming season.

Old Garden Rose bushes have a shrubby growth that survives well in poorer soil with less sun, and require little maintenance. Old Garden Roses fit well in natural garden borders and when planted near foundations and garden walls. Although they only bloom once a year, the bushes are covered with flowers that look best when

Antique vs. Modern Roses

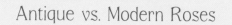

they are fully open. Perhaps the best quality of most Old Garden Roses is their pungent and varied perfume.

Hybrid Tea Roses have larger, more perfect blooms with graceful pointed buds, and some varieties have fragrance. They grow upright and can be pruned into tree shapes, so they are most showy in beds and borders. The Hybrid Tea Roses are available in myriad colors and will repeat bloom—providing flowers over the spring and summer. They are more tolerant of cold weather than Old Garden Roses, but require careful and constant attention to sun and soil quality, feeding, spraying, and pruning.

If you want roses that require little attention and smell wonderful, and if you admire the loose and wilder look of the flower, Old Garden Roses are for you. But if you want perfect blooms in a rainbow of colors and are willing to spend time caring for them, choose from the hundreds of Hybrid Tea Roses for your garden. Both roses are beautiful when cut, the Old ones will perfume a room, but the Teas have longer stems and will last longer when you bring them inside.

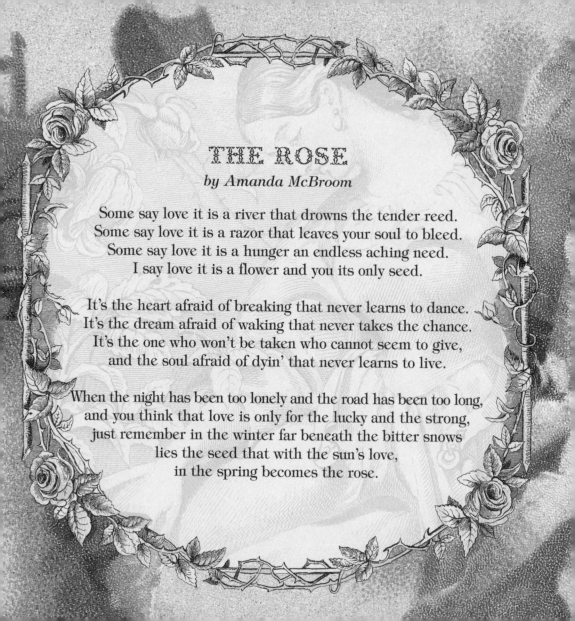

THE ROSE

by Amanda McBroom

Some say love it is a river that drowns the tender reed.
Some say love it is a razor that leaves your soul to bleed.
Some say love it is a hunger an endless aching need.
I say love it is a flower and you its only seed.

It's the heart afraid of breaking that never learns to dance.
It's the dream afraid of waking that never takes the chance.
It's the one who won't be taken who cannot seem to give,
and the soul afraid of dyin' that never learns to live.

When the night has been too lonely and the road has been too long,
and you think that love is only for the lucky and the strong,
just remember in the winter far beneath the bitter snows
lies the seed that with the sun's love,
in the spring becomes the rose.

One Perfect Rose

A single flow'r he sent me, since we met.
All tenderly his messenger he chose;
Deep-hearted, pure, with scented dew still wet—
One perfect rose.

I knew the language of the floweret;
"My fragile leaves," it said, "his heart enclose."
Love long has taken for his amulet
One perfect rose.

Why is it no one ever sent yet
One perfect limousine, do you suppose?
Ah no, it's always just my luck to get
One perfect rose.

—DOROTHY PARKER

The Legend of the Christmas Rose

by Selma Lagerlöf

Robber Mother, who lived in Robbers' Cave up in Göinge forest, went down to the village one day on a begging tour. Robber Father, who was an outlawed man, did not dare to leave the forest. She took with her five youngsters, and each youngster bore a sack on his back as long as himself. When Robber Mother stepped inside the door of a cabin, no one dared refuse to give her whatever she demanded; for she was not above coming back the following night and setting fire to the house if she had not been well received. Robber Mother and her brood were worse than a pack of wolves, and many a man felt like running a spear through them; but it was never done, because they all knew that the man stayed up in the forest, and he would have known how to wreak vengeance if anything had happened to the children or the old woman.

Now that Robber Mother went from house to house and begged, she came to Övid, which at that time was a cloister. She rang the bell of the cloister gate and asked for food. The watchman let down a small wicket in the gate and handed her six round bread cakes—one for herself and one for each of the five children.

While the mother was standing quietly at the gate, her youngsters were running about. And now one of them came and pulled at her skirt, as a

The Legend of the Christmas Rose

signal that he had discovered something which she ought to come and see, and Robber Mother followed him promptly.

The entire cloister was surrounded by a high and strong wall, but the youngster had managed to find a little back gate which stood ajar. When Robber Mother got there, she pushed the gate open and walked inside without asking leave, as it was her custom to do.

Övid Cloister was managed at that time by Abbot Hans, who knew all about herbs. Just within the cloister wall he had planted a little herb garden, and it was into this that the old woman had forced her way.

At first glance Robber Mother was so astonished that she paused at the gate. It was high summertide, and Abbot Hans' garden was so full of flowers that the eyes were fairly dazzled by the blues, reds, and yellows, as one looked into it. But presently an indulgent smile spread over her features, and she started to walk up a narrow path that lay between many flower beds.

In the garden a lay brother walked about, pulling up weeds. It was he who had left the door in the wall open, that he might throw the weeds and tares on the rubbish heap outside.

When he saw Robber

The Legend of the Christmas Rose

Mother coming in, with all five youngsters in tow, he ran toward her at once and ordered them away. But the beggar woman walked right on as before. The lay brother knew of no other remedy than to run into the cloister and call for help.

He returned with two stalwart monks, and Robber Mother saw that now it meant business! She let out a perfect volley of shrieks, and, throwing herself upon the monks, clawed and bit at them; so did all the youngsters. The men soon learned that she could overpower them, and all they could do was go back into the cloister for reinforcements.

As they ran through the passage-way which led to the cloister, they met Abbot Hans, who came rushing out to learn what all this noise was about.

He upbraided them for using force and forbade their calling for help. He sent both monks back to their work, and although he was an old and fragile man, he took with him only the lay brother.

He came up to the woman and asked in a mild tone if the garden pleased her.

Robber Mother turned defiantly toward Abbot Hans, for she expected only to be trapped and over-powered. But when she noticed his white hair and bent form, she answered peaceably, "First, when I saw this, I thought I had never seen a prettier garden; but now I see that it can't be compared with one I know of. If you could see the garden of which I am thinking you would uproot all the flowers planted here and cast them away like weeds."

The Abbot's assistant was hardly less proud of the flowers than the Abbot himself, and after hearing her remarks he laughed derisively.

Robber Mother grew crimson with rage to think that her word was doubted, and she cried out: "You monks, who are holy men, certainly must know that on every Christmas Eve the great Göinge forest is transformed into a beautiful garden, to commemorate the hour of our Lord's birth. We who live in the forest have seen this happen every year. And in that garden I have seen flowers so lovely that I dared not lift my hand to pluck them."

Ever since his childhood, Abbot Hans had heard it said that on every Christmas Eve the forest was dressed in holiday glory. He had often longed to see it, but he had never had the good fortune. Eagerly he begged and implored Robber Mother that he might come up to the Robbers' Cave on Christmas Eve. If she would only send one of her children to show him the way, he could ride up there alone, and he would never betray them—on the contrary, he would reward them insofar as it lay in his power.

Robber Mother said no at first, for she was thinking of Robber Father

The Legend of the Christmas Rose

and of the peril which might befall him should she permit Abbot Hans to ride up to their cave. At the same time the desire to prove to the monk that the garden which she knew was more beautiful than his got the better of her, and she gave in.

"But more than one follower you cannot take with you," said she, "and you are not to waylay us or trap us, as sure as you are a holy man."

This Abbot Hans promised, and then Robber Mother went her way.

It happened that Archbishop Absalon from Lund came to Övid and remained through the night. The lay brother heard Abbot Hans telling the Bishop about Robber Father and asking him for a letter of ransom for the man, that he might lead an honest life among respectable folk.

But the Archbishop replied that he did not care to let the robber loose among honest folk in the villages. It would be best for all that he remain in the forest.

Then Abbot Hans grew zealous and told the Bishop all about Göinge forest, which, every year at Yuletide, clothed itself in summer bloom around the Robbers' Cave. "If these bandits are not so bad but that God's glories can be made manifest to them, surely we cannot be too wicked to experience the same blessing."

The Archbishop knew how to answer Abbot Hans. "This much I will promise you, Abbot Hans," he said, smiling, "that any day you send me a blossom from the garden in Göinge forest, I will give you letters of ransom for all the outlaws you may choose to plead for."

The Legend of the Christmas Rose

The following Christmas Eve Abbot Hans was on his way to the forest. One of the Robber Mother's wild youngsters ran ahead of him, and close behind him was the lay brother.

It turned out to be a long and hazardous ride. They climbed steep and slippery side paths, crawled over swamp and marsh, and pushed through windfall and bramble. Just as daylight was waning, the robber boy guided them across a forest meadow, skirted by tall, naked leaf trees and green fir trees. Back of the meadow loomed a mountain wall, and in this wall they saw a door of thick boards. Now Abbot Hans understood that they had arrived, and dismounted. The child opened the heavy door for him, and he looked into a poor mountain grotto, with bare stone walls. Robber Mother was seated before a log fire that burned in the middle of the floor. Alongside the walls were beds of virgin pine and moss, and on one of these beds lay Robber Father asleep.

"Come in, you out there!" shouted Robber Mother without rising, "and fetch the horses in with you, so they won't be destroyed by the night cold."

Abbot Hans walked boldly into the cave, and the lay brother followed. Here were wretchedness and poverty! and nothing was done to celebrate Christmas.

Robber Mother spoke in a tone as haughty and dictatorial as any well-to-do peasant woman. "Sit down by the fire and warm yourself, Abbot Hans," said she; "and if you have food with you, eat, for the food which

The Legend of the Christmas Rose

we in the forest prepare you wouldn't care to taste. And if you
are tired after the long journey, you can lie down on one of these
beds to sleep. You needn't be afraid of oversleeping, for I'm sitting here
by the fire keeping watch. I shall awaken you in time to see that which
you have come up here to see."

Abbot Hans obeyed Robber Mother and brought forth his food sack;
but he was so fatigued after the journey he was hardly able to eat, and as
soon as he could stretch himself on the bed, he fell asleep.

The lay brother was also assigned a bed to rest and he dropped into
a doze.

When he woke up, he saw that Abbot Hans had left his bed and was
sitting by the fire talking with Robber Mother. The outlawed robber sat
also by the fire. He was a tall, raw-boned man with a dull,
sluggish appearance. His back was turned to Abbot
Hans, as though he would have it appear that he
was not listening to the conversation.

Abbot Hans was telling Robber
Mother all about the Christmas
preparations he had seen on
the journey, reminding
her of Christmas
feasts and games
which she must have

The Legend of the Christmas Rose

known in her youth, when she lived at peace with mankind.

At first Robber Mother answered in short, gruff sentences, but by degrees she became more subdued and listened more intently. Suddenly Robber Father turned toward Abbot Hans and shook his clenched fist in his face. "You miserable monk! did you come here to coax from me my wife and children? Don't you know that I am an outlaw and may not leave the forest?"

Abbot Hans looked him fearlessly in the eyes. "It is my purpose to get a letter of ransom for you from Archbishop Absalon," said he. He had hardly finished speaking when the robber and his wife burst out laughing. They knew well enough the kind of mercy a forest robber could expect from Bishop Absalon!

"Oh, if I get a letter of ransom from Absalon," said Robber Father, "then I'll promise you that never again will I steal so much as a goose."

Suddenly Robber Mother rose. "You sit here and talk, Abbot Hans," she said, "so that we are forgetting to look at the forest. Now I can hear, even in this cave, how the Christmas bells are ringing."

The words were barely uttered when they all sprang up and rushed out. But in the forest it was still dark night and bleak winter. The only thing they marked was a distant clang borne on a light south wind.

When the bells had been ringing a few moments, a sudden illumination penetrated the forest; the next moment it was dark again, and then light came back. It pushed its way forward between the stark trees, like a

The Legend of the Christmas Rose

shimmering mist. The darkness merged into a faint daybreak.

Then Abbot Hans saw that the snow had vanished from the ground, as if someone had removed a carpet, and the earth began to take on a green covering. The moss-tufts thickened and raised themselves, and the spring blossoms shot upward their swelling buds, which already had a touch of color.

Again it grew hazy; but almost immediately there came a new wave of light. Then the leaves of the trees burst into bloom, crossbeaks hopped from branch to branch, and the woodpeckers hammered on the limbs until the splinters fairly flew around them. A flock of starlings from up country lighted in a fir top to rest.

When the next warm wind came along, the blueberries ripened and the baby squirrels began playing on the branches of the trees.

The next light wave that came rushing in brought with it the scent of newly ploughed acres. Pine and spruce trees were so thickly clothed with red cones that they shone like crimson mantles and forest flowers covered the ground till it was all red, blue, and yellow.

Abbot Hans bent down to the earth and broke off a wild strawberry blossom, and, as he straightened up, the berry ripened in his hand.

The mother fox came out of her lair with a big litter of black-legged young. She went up to Robber Mother and scratched at her skirt, and Robber Mother bent down to her and praised her young.

Robber Mother's youngsters let out perfect shrieks of delight. They stuffed themselves with wild strawberries that hung on the bushes.

One of them played with a litter of young hares; another ran a race with some young crows, which had hopped from their nest before they were really ready.

Robber Father was standing out on a marsh eating raspberries. When he glanced up, a big black bear stood beside him. Robber Father broke off a twig and struck the bear on the nose. "Keep to your own ground, you!" he said; "this is my turf." The huge bear turned around and lumbered off in another direction.

Then all the flowers whose seeds had been brought from foreign lands began to blossom. The loveliest roses climbed up the mountain wall in a race with the blackberry vines, and from the forest meadow sprang flowers as large as human faces.

Abbot Hans thought of the flower he was to pluck for Bishop Absalon; but each new flower that appeared was more beautiful than the others, and he wanted to choose the most beautiful of all.

Then Abbot Hans

marked how all grew still; the birds hushed their songs, the flowers ceased growing, and the young foxes played no more. From far in the distance faint harp tones were heard, and celestial song, like a soft murmur, reached him.

He clasped his hands and dropped to his knees. His face was radiant with bliss.

But beside Abbot Hans stood the lay brother who had accompanied him. In his mind there were dark thoughts. "This cannot be a true miracle," he thought, "since it is revealed to malefactors. This does not come from God, but is sent hither by Satan. It is the Evil One's power that is tempting us and compelling us to see that which has no real existence."

The angel throng was so near now that Abbot Hans saw their bright forms through the forest branches. The lay brother saw them, too; but back of all this wondrous beauty he saw only some dread evil.

All the while the birds had been circling around the head of Abbot Hans, and they let him take them in his hands. But all the animals were afraid of the lay brother; no bird perched on his shoulder, no snake played at his feet. Then there came a little forest dove. When she marked that the angels were nearing, she plucked up courage and flew down on the lay brother's shoulder and laid her head against his cheek.

Then it appeared to him as if sorcery were come right upon him, to tempt and corrupt him. He struck with his hand at the forest dove and cried in such a loud voice that it rang throughout the forest, "Go thou

back to hell, whence thou are come!"

Just then the angels were so near that Abbot Hans felt the feathery touch of their great wings, and he bowed down to earth in reverent greeting.

But when the lay brother's words sounded, their song was hushed and the holy guests turned in flight. At the same time the light and the mild warmth vanished in unspeakable terror for the darkness and cold in a human heart. Darkness sank over the earth, like a coverlet; frost came, all the growths shriveled up; the animals and birds hastened away; the leaves dropped from the trees, rustling like rain.

Abbot Hans felt how his heart, which had but lately swelled with bliss, was now contracting with insufferable agony. "I can never outlive this," thought he, "that the angels from heaven had been so close to me and were driven away; that they wanted to sing Christmas carols for me and were driven to flight."

Then he remembered the flower he had promised Bishop Absalon, and at the last moment he fumbled among the leaves and moss to try and find a blossom. But he sensed how the ground under his fingers froze and how the white snow came gliding over the ground. Then his heart caused him even greater anguish. He could not rise, but fell prostrate on the ground and lay there.

When the robber folk and the lay brother had groped their way back to the cave, they missed Abbot Hans. They took brands with them and went out to search for him. The found him dead upon the coverlet of snow.

When Abbot Hans had been carried down to Övid, those who took charge of the dead saw that he held his right hand locked tight around something which he must have grasped at the moment of death. When they finally got his hand open, they found that the thing which he had held in such an iron grip was a pair of white root bulbs, which he had torn from among the moss and leaves.

When the lay brother who had accompanied Abbot Hans saw the bulbs, he took them and planted them in Abbot Hans' herb garden.

He guarded them the whole year to see if any flower would spring from them. But in vain he waited through the spring, the summer, and the autumn. Finally, when winter had set in and all the leaves and the flowers were dead, he ceased caring for them.

But when Christmas Eve came again, he was so strongly reminded of Abbot Hans that he wandered out into the garden to think of him. And look! as he came to the spot where he had planted the bare root bulbs, he saw that from them had

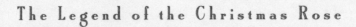

sprung flourishing green stalks, which bore beautiful flowers
with silver white leaves.

He called out all the monks at Övid, and when they saw that this plant
bloomed on Christmas Eve, when all the other growths were as if dead,
they understood that this flower had in truth been plucked by Abbot
Hans from the Christmas garden in Göinge forest. Then the lay brother
asked the monks if he might
take a few blossoms to Bishop Absalon.

When Bishop Absalon beheld the flowers,
which had spring from the earth in darkest winter, he turned as pale as if
he had met a ghost. He sat in silence a moment; thereupon he said,
"Abbot Hans has faithfully kept his word and I shall also keep mine."

He handed the letter of ransom to the lay brother, who departed at
once for the Robbers' Cave. When he stepped in there on Christmas Day,
the robber came toward him with axe uplifted. "I'd like to hack you
monks into bits, as many as you are!" said he. "It must be your fault
that Göinge forest did not last night dress itself in Christmas bloom."

"The fault is mine alone," said the lay brother, "and I will gladly die
for it; but first I must deliver a message from Abbot Hans." And he drew
forth the Bishop's letter and told the man that he was free.

Robber Father stood there pale and speechless, but Robber Mother
said in his name, "Abbot Hans has indeed kept his word, and Robber
Father will keep his."

The Legend of the Christmas Rose

When the robber and his wife left the cave, the lay brother moved in and lived all alone in the forest, in constant meditation and prayer that his hard-heartedness might be forgiven him.

But Göinge forest never again celebrated the hour of our Savior's birth; and of all its glory, there lives today only the plant which Abbot Hans had plucked. It has been named CHRISTMAS ROSE. And each year at Christmastide she sends forth from the earth her green stalks and white blossoms, as if she never could forget that she had once grown in the great Christmas garden at Göinge forest.

If thou canst get but thither,
There grows the flower of peace,
The rose that cannot wither,
Thy fortress and thy ease.

—Henry Vaughan

The Bowl of Roses

And the movement in the roses, look:
gestures from such small angles of deflection
that they'd remain invisible, if their
rays did not fan out into the universe.
Look at that white one which blissfully unfolded
and stands there in the great open petals
like a Venus upright in the seashell;
and the blushing one, which as if confused
turns across to one that is cool,
and how that cold one stands, wrapped in itself,
among the open ones that shed everything.
And what they shed: how it can be
light and heavy, a cloak, a burden, a wing
and a mask, it varies endlessly,
and how they shed it: as before the loved one.

What can't they be: was that yellow one,
which lies there hollow and open, not the rind
of a fruit, in which the very same yellow,
more collected, orange-redder, was juice?
And was opening-out too much for this one,
since in the air its indescribable pink
took on the bitter aftertaste of violet?
And that cambric one, is it not a dress
in which, still soft and breath-warm, the chemise
clings, both of them cast off at once
in the morning shadows of the old forest pool?
And this one, opalescent porcelain,
fragile, a shallow china cup
and filled with tiny bright butterflies,—
and that one, which contains nothing but itself.

And aren't all that way, containing just themselves,
if self-containing means: to change the world outside
and wind and rain and patience of the spring
and guilt and restlessness and muffled fate
and the darkness of the evening earth
out to the changing and flying and fleeing of the cloud
and the vague influence of distant stars
into a hand full of inwardness.

Now it lies carefree in these open roses.

—RAINER MARIA RILKE

Caring for Cut Roses

*S*ay you've just received a beautiful arrangement of florist's roses, or decided to treat yourself from a less-expensive flower stand. How can you preserve them for as long as possible and keep them from wilting within 24 hours? Follow these tips, and caring for your fresh roses will be a snap.

❧

If you can, buy your roses from a trusted florist—the quality of the blooms will be better to start with. And don't be afraid to ask your florist which flowers are the freshest that day.

❧

Ask about the vase life of the rose variety you want; some varieties naturally last longer than others. If you are intending to arrange your roses with other flowers, you also should ask your florist which flowers are most compatible. Some flowers secrete sap that could cause your roses to wilt even faster.

❧

Make sure you remove leaves below the water line in the vase. Submerged foliage contributes to bacteria growth that will wilt your roses.

❧

Caring for Cut Roses

Keep your roses from getting thirsty! Use pruning shears or a sharp knife—scissors will crush the stems—and cut at least an inch off the bottom of each rose at a 45-degree angle. Keep the stems submerged while cutting to prevent air bubbles from penetrating the stem and blocking the intake of water. Then place them in a vase of fresh warm water.

❧

Ask for plenty of floral preservative to add to the vase water as you change it. It gives the roses the food they need and helps keep bacteria at bay.

❧

Change the water daily and trim your rose stems every few days.

❧

To revive a wilted bloom: Cut another inch off the stem and place in fresh water with preservative. If that doesn't work, try submerging the entire rose and stem in cool water for an hour.

❧

Display roses in a cool area of your home, away from direct sunlight, drafts, or heat sources. This will help blooms stay at their loveliest for as long as possible.

Rose Petal Scones

2 CUPS ALL-PURPOSE FLOUR,
PLUS EXTRA FOR DUSTING

$1/2$ CUP SUGAR

2 TEASPOONS BAKING POWDER

$1/4$ TEASPOON BAKING SODA

6 TABLESPOONS COLD BUTTER,
CUT INTO SMALL PIECES

$1/2$ CUP CURRANTS (OPTIONAL)

2 TABLESPOONS FRESHLY GRATED
ORANGE RIND (ABOUT ONE
LARGE ORANGE)

$1/2$ CUP BUTTERMILK

1 TEASPOON ROSE WATER
(SEE P. 68 FOR RECIPE)

$1/4$ CUP ORGANIC ROSE PETALS,
CHOPPED

1 TABLESPOON GROUND CINNAMON

2 TABLESPOONS SUGAR

1. Preheat oven to 375°F. In a large bowl, mix flour, sugar, baking powder, and baking soda.
2. Add butter. With pastry blender, two forks, or your fingers, work the butter into the dry ingredients until mixture resembles course crumbs. Stir in currants and orange rind.
3. Make a well in the center of the dough and pour in buttermilk, rose water, and rose petals. Using your hands or a fork, gently combine until dough holds

together. With lightly floured hands, (dough will be sticky) knead dough on a floured board for 5 or 6 turns.

4. Shape dough into a smooth ball. With knife, cut dough into quarters. With pancake turner, place scones, 2 inches apart, on a greased cookie sheet.

5. Combine cinnamon and remaining sugar. Sprinkle half over unbaked scones. Bake 10 minutes and then sprinkle with remaining cinnamon sugar. Bake another 20 minutes or until golden brown. Serve warm, or remove from cookie sheet and cool on wire rack to reheat later.

Yields four scones.

This bud of love, by
Summer's ripening breath
May prove a beauteous
Flower when next we meet.

—William Shakespeare

Little Women

by Louisa May Alcott

When the evening for the "small party" came, she found that the poplin wouldn't do at all, for the other girls were putting on thin dresses and making themselves very fine indeed; so out came the tartalan, looking older, limper, and shabbier than ever beside Sallie's crisp new one. Meg saw the girls glance at it and then one another, and her cheeks began to burn, for with all her gentleness she was very proud. No one said a word about it, but Sallie offered to dress her hair, and Annie to tie her sash, and Belle, the engaged sister, praised her white arms; but in their kindness Meg saw only pity for her poverty, and her heart felt very heavy as she stood by herself, while the others laughed, chattered, and flew about like gauzy butterflies. The hard, bitter feeling was getting pretty bad, when the maid brought in a box of flowers. Before she could speak, Annie had the cover off, and all were exclaiming at the lovely roses, heath, and ferns within.

"It's for Belle, of course; George always sends her some, but these are altogether ravishing," cried Annie, with a great sniff.

"They are for Miss March," the man said.

"And here's a note," put in the maid, holding it to Meg.

"What fun! Who are they from? Didn't know you had a lover,"

cried the girls, fluttering about Meg in a high state of curiosity and surprise.

"The note is from mother, and the flowers from Laurie," said Meg, simply, yet much gratified that he had not forgotten her.

"Oh indeed!" said Annie, with a funny look, as Meg slipped the note into her pocket, as a sort of talisman against envy, vanity, and false pride; for the few loving words had done her good, and the flowers cheered her up by their beauty.

Feeling almost happy again, she laid by a few ferns and roses for herself, and quickly made up the rest in dainty bouquets for the breasts, hair, or skirts of her friends, offering them so prettily that Clara, the elder sister, told her she was "the sweetest little thing she ever saw," and they looked quite charmed with her small attention. Somehow the kind act finished her despondency; and when all the rest went to show themselves to Mrs. Moffat, she saw a happy, bright-eyed face in the mirror, as she laid her ferns against her rippling hair and fastened the roses in the dress that didn't strike her as so *very* shabby now.

To A Friend who Sent Me

As late I rambled in the happy fields,
What time the skylark shakes the
tremulous dew
From his lush clover covert;—
when anew
Adventurous knights take up their
dinted shields:
I saw the sweetest flower wild nature
yields,
A fresh-blown musk-rose; 'twas
the first that threw
Its sweets upon the summer:
graceful it grew

Some Roses

As is the wand that Queen Titania wields.
And, as I feasted on its fragrancy,
 I thought the garden rose it far
 excelled:
But when, O Wells! thy roses came to me
 My sense with their deliciousness was
 spelled:
Soft voices had they, that with tender plea
 Whispered of peace, and truth and
 friendliness
  unquelled.

—JOHN KEATS

Celebrity Roses

Many rose breeders look for attention-grabbing names for their new offspring, one that will attract gardeners and boost sales. What could be better than naming your rose after a celebrity? These roses aspire to reflect the best aspects of their namesakes.

GRACIE ALLEN
Floribunda rose with small white blooms
tinted with light pink

LYNN ANDERSON
Hybrid tea rose in cream edged with deep pink

LUCILLE BALL
Apricot-colored hybrid tea rose

INGRID BERGMAN
Rich red hybrid tea rose

BETTY BOOP
Floribunda rose with a yellow to cream center and red edges

GEORGE BURNS
Floribunda with yellow-and-red-striped blooms

Celebrity Roses

BARBARA BUSH
Coral pink hybrid tea rose

ROSALYN CARTER
Floribunda with coral, red, and orange flowers

PATSY CLINE
Hybrid tea rose in cream to deep pink

BING CROSBY
Orange hybrid tea rose

LEONARDO DA VINCI
Floribunda with light pink flowers

CARDINAL DE RICHELIEU
Gallica rose with velvety purple blooms

PRINCESS DIANA
Ivory hybrid tea rose with a clear pink blush

QUEEN ELIZABETH
Pink floribunda rose

CHRIS EVERT
Melon orange hybrid tea rose with a red blush

HENRY FONDA
Deep yellow hybrid tea rose

GIVENCHY
Pink hybrid tea rose with cream and yellow in the heart

WHOOPI GOLDBERG
Miniature hybrid tea rose with red and white flowers

Celebrity Roses

BILLY GRAHAM
Clear pink hybrid tea rose

CARY GRANT
Reddish-orange hybrid
tea rose

AUDREY HEPBURN
Hybrid tea rose in
apple blossom pink

BOB HOPE
Cherry red hybrid
tea rose

GERTRUDE JEKYLL
(noted gardener)
Bright pink English
garden rose

DON JUAN
Dark red bourbon
climbing rose

JOHN F. KENNEDY
Bright white hybrid
tea rose

ANGELA LANSBURY
Hybrid tea rose in light
pink with cream

PRESIDENT LINCOLN
Deep pink bourbon rose

REBA MCINTIRE
Grandiflora rose in
orange-red

MICHELANGELO
Hybrid tea romantica rose
in bright yellow

**PRINCESS GRACE
OF MONACO**
Ivory hybrid tea rose
edged in cherry pink

Celebrity Roses

MARILYN MONROE
Apricot cream hybrid tea
rose washed with green

ROSIE O'DONNELL
Pure red hybrid tea rose
with yellow-backed petals

DOLLY PARTON
Rich red-orange hybrid
tea rose

MINNIE PEARL
Miniature rose in ivory
blushed with salmon

PINOCCHIO
Bushy lavender-pink
floribunda rose

ST. PATRICK
Pale yellow hybrid tea rose
with greenish outer petals

LEE ANN RIMES
Hybrid tea rose with
creamy yellow centers
and pink edges

BARBRA STREISAND
Cool, lavender hybrid
tea rose

ELIZABETH TAYLOR
Deep pink hybrid tea rose
with smoky edges

SHAKESPEARE'S ROSE
Pale pink wild species rose

SNOW WHITE
Beautiful bright white
hybrid tea rose

The sweetest flower that blows,
I give you as we part.
For you it is a rose,
For me it is my heart.

—Frederick Peterson

The White Flag

I sent my love two roses,—one
    As white as driven snow,
And one a blushing royal red,
    A flaming Jacqueminot . . . .

My heart sank when I met her: sure
    I had been overbold,
For on her breast my pale rose lay
    In virgin whiteness cold.

Yet with low words she greeted me,
    With smiles divinely tender;
Upon her cheek the red rose dawned,—
    The white rose meant surrender.

—JOHN HAY

Pruning Your Roses

Pruning is essential for the health of your roses. Once-blooming roses need little pruning: cut out the deadwood in late winter, then cut canes back by a third after flowering. For continuous-flowering roses, cut back deadwood in late winter and remove one or two old canes at the base to encourage new growth. Cut back the rest by a third, and deadhead continuously during the summer to encourage blooms. Some roses require more attention than others, but the following tips offer good general pruning guidelines for all.

❧

HAVE THE RIGHT TOOLS FOR THE JOB: Clean, sharp pruners and loppers make all the difference. Use pruners for shoots up to a half inch in diameter and loppers for canes up to an inch. Use the pruning saw for any jobs larger than that. Be sure to sterilize your tools after each use to prevent the spread of disease. Mix two tablespoons of bleach to a quart of water, and rinse tools after use.

❧

REMOVE DEADWOOD: Your rose canes will be green even in the winter, except for very old growth. To recognize deadwood, look for canes that are grayish brown and have discolored tissue below the surface when scratched. If the cane has completely died, prune

Pruning Your Roses

it all the way back to the ground. If the deadwood has spread only partway down the cane, make a clean cut through live wood at least a half inch below the lowest point of damage.

☙

REMOVE DISEASED OR DAMAGED WOOD: If you see evidence of canker, rust, or other diseases, pruning could prevent further damage. Cut out canes afflicted with canker well below the damaged wood, and be sure to sterilize your tools to prevent the spread of disease.

☙

BEWARE ROOTSTOCK SUCKERS! If your roses grow on grafted rootstock, watch out for alien suckers. These shoots will have a different look from the rest of your rose, and the leaves may have a slightly different color and shape. In basic terms, the rootstock is putting up its own shoots, and if they are not removed, the rose plant grown from the graft will die off and the rootstock rose will take over. Remove these suckers at the source by digging down to the root, and pulling them off. Don't snip them with your pruners: That will only encourage more growth!

☙

Pruning Your Roses

SHARPEN YOUR TOOLS. Make the kindest cuts to your plants by sharpening your tools once a year. Sharp tools allow you to make cuts cleanly, which promotes new growth.

&

CUT JUST ABOVE A NEW BUD: Make the cut on a 45-degree angle about an eighth of an inch above an outward facing bud. Slant the cut upward and outward over the bud. Pruning close to the bud will encourage new growth, and cutting on an angle will allow rainwater to run off the stem and prevent disease.

&

TRIM CANES THAT CROSS EACH OTHER: Canes that cross-rub create abrasions that allow disease to enter. Pruning out crossed canes also promotes air circulation, which deters dreaded mold and mildew.

&

PRUNE OUT WEAK AND SKINNY GROWTH: These canes are simply sucking the energy from your plants, leaving less of it to produce flowers. They probably will not develop buds of their own, so it is best to just remove them.

&

NEVER COMPOST YOUR ROSE CLIPPINGS: Discard or burn all cuttings because they can harbor fungus and disease. Rake up any fallen rose leaves as well, to keep pests and mildew at bay.

Rose Vinegar

*A time-honored recipe that dates
back nearly 400 years.*

1 CUP PINK ORGANIC ROSE PETALS
2 SPRIGS OF FRESH TARRAGON
1 LITER DISTILLED WHITE SALAD VINEGAR

Mix rose petals, tarragon, and vinegar together
in a jar. Seal tightly and let sit for three weeks.
Strain petals and tarragon from vinegar.
Pour rose vinegar into glass bottle.

Little Known Rose Facts

An ancient creation legend states that in the Garden of Eden, all the roses had no thorns. It was only after the expulsion of Adam and Eve from the garden that the thorns appeared.

Another creation story tells of the lily and the white rose. Both flowered in the Garden of Eden, and Adam asked Eve which flower was more beautiful. Eve asked the angel Gabriel for his advice. Gabriel preferred the lily, as he had pricked himself on the thorns of the rose while trying to pick a flower. The rose, greatly offended, left the garden when Adam and Eve were driven out, as her fragrance should have been reward enough.

Little Known Rose Facts

Although Vincent Van Gogh is known for painting sunflowers and irises, he also painted at least eleven works featuring roses.

Roses are native to the United States. The oldest fossilized rose was found in Florissant, Colorado and is estimated to be 35 million years old.

Arabs used roses extensively in the Middle Ages, sprinkling rosewater in mosques and, even today, adding it to desserts. Rosewater was combined with gum arabic to make prayer beads.

Roses and their hips have long been valued for their medicinal properties. Napoleon's army even used rose petals boiled in white wine to treat lead poisoning from bullet wounds.

There should be beds of Roses,
banks of Roses, bowers of Roses,
hedges of Roses, edgings of Roses,
pillars of Roses, arches of Roses,
fountains of Roses, baskets of Roses,
vistas and alleys of the Rose.

—Dean Hole

Flowers

The cowslip is a country wench,
The violet is a nun;
But I will woo the dainty rose,
The queen of everyone.

—THOMAS HOOD

TEXT CREDITS

ILLUSTRATION CREDITS